Donuts, Antiques and Murder

A Bakery Detectives Cozy Mystery

By

Stacey Alabaster

Table of Contents

Introduction

Thank you so much for buying my book. I am excited to share my stories with you and hope that you are just as thrilled to read them.

If you would like to know about all my new releases and have the opportunity to get free books, make sure you sign up for our Cozy Mystery Newsletter.

FairfieldPublishing.com/cozy-newsletter

Stacey Alabaster

Chapter 1

Blood red jam seeped out as I pressed down on the pastry, causing it to drip from the center of the donut.

The smell of fresh cinnamon sugar sprinkled all over the donut hit my nose. *I need to taste test it for the good of the business,* I justified to myself before I popped the soft, warm donut in my mouth. *Mmm.*

I started coughing and Pippa had to thump my back as the first customers of the day started to pour into my shop, Rachael's Boutique Bakery. I straightened up and put on my brightest smile, my eyes still watering from my near-choke-experience. It probably served me right. I looked down at the trays of jam donuts and then at the line of early bird customers. We'd be lucky if we had enough to last the morning rush.

One after another they came, flooding the shop and making my heart leap for joy. Only a few months earlier I had thought my poor little bakery was going to perish, but now it was flourishing more than ever before.

Only one little teeny tiny problem: success can lead to complacency. Worse than that, it can lead to boredom.

My fingers were itching, and not just to knead dough, but to solve a mystery.

"Oi!" Pippa reached over and gave me a playful shove. "Stop daydreaming about solving mysteries!" Her hair was bright blue this month and it was often a talking point for customers when they came into the shop. "It's blueberry," she would say with a wink, before trying to sell them one of our fresh blueberry muffins. At least she was creative.

"I'm not," I said, standing up quickly, embarrassed. "That's all in the past. I'm one hundred percent focused on the bakery now."

Pippa shot me a skeptical look as a lock of bright blue hair fell into her eyes. "Doesn't look that way to me." She took off her apron, the morning rush over, and began to count the money in the cash register, one of her new tasks as assistant manager. "Besides," she said with a cheeky lift of her brow. "You know I've got plenty of real mysteries for you to solve, if you're into paranormal stuff."

I groaned. "I wouldn't call those 'real' mysteries, Pippa. I wish you'd stop hanging out with those people." I couldn't care less about hunting cryptoids or chasing ghosts, or whatever it was that Pippa and her new friends were into. I'd had a taste of the real thing; solved a real life murder. And, although I've never wish for harm to fall on anyone, I couldn't help missing the rush that had come with being an amateur detective. Belldale had been quiet—and, yes, boring—for the past two months.

"Our best morning yet!" Pippa announced with glee as she pushed the register closed again. "A new record."

We high-fived and I grinned.

Sure, solving mysteries was fun, but it didn't put money in the bank. The bakery did. I had to remember that.

Besides, a new record day meant I could finally take the plunge and do something even more exciting than solving a murder mystery.

I took a deep breath and followed Pippa over to an empty table as she took her break. I let her eat anything she liked on break and today she had chosen a Danish pastry.

"Guess what, Pippa?" I sat across from her, too excited to eat anything as I readied myself to tell her the exciting news.

I could see her mind already starting to work as she

looked up at the ceiling and poked her tongue out of the corner of her mouth.

"Hmm, you're finally going on a date with Detective Whitaker!"

"Pippa! No! Don't be silly."

"Well, has he called you yet?"

"Pippa...no...that doesn't matter. That's not my news and I wouldn't be excited about it if it were. Keep guessing."

She put her Danish down and chewed on it, still pondering.

"You've found another mystery to solve? Is that it? I know that would make you excited."

I shook my head. "That's not it."

She threw her hands in the air and said she was ready to give up. "Besides, cookies need to come out of the oven," she said, hurrying over to the oven to pull out the tray before she gave one last wild guess. "You've won the lottery?"

"Nope!" I said, pleased that she hadn't guessed. "Pippa, we're expanding the bakery. I'm purchasing the antiques shop next door!"

The tray of cookies she was carrying crashed to the ground.

Not exactly the reaction I was hoping for. Was she happy? Excited? Her wide eyes said otherwise.

"Rachael," Pippa whispered as she gripped the collar of my shirt. "You can't purchase the antiques shop!" Her face was as white as a ghost.

"Pippa!" I shook her off and brushed at my shirt. "Why-ever not? I thought you would be pleased for me? For us." Pippa had a...let's just say 'issue' keeping a job longer than a week. Her tenure at my bakery, two months now, was the longest she had ever stayed at a job. I thought she would be thrilled to know that she had secure employment in a blossoming business.

"I'm pleased that the bakery is successful." Pippa stopped and glanced over her shoulder in the direction of the antiques shop, as though she could see through the brick wall. She shook her head slowly. "But you can't buy the shop next door." She turned back to face me, her eyes still as wide as pies.

"Rachael, that place is haunted."

I scoffed. "Oh, come on, Pippa. I know you believe a lot of outlandish things, but this is too much."

"Rachael!" Her voice was high and indignant. "You must have heard the rumors."

I walked back to the counter in a little bit of a huff. I felt as though Pippa was raining on my parade. "No, I haven't heard any rumors." I shot Pippa a look. "But I don't really frequent the same places you do."

I was talking about the Belldale Haunted House tour and the Belldale Paranormal Club. Pippa had recently joined and had attended several of their tours, which took place after dark and involved dragging locals and tourists alike around Belldale's 'most haunted' locations. Pippa had come back to our apartment following these tours and given me several breathless accounts of how amazing and eye-opening they were, while I tried to listen with a straight face.

Pippa let out a deep sigh. "Well, yes, the haunted house tour *was* very informative when it came to the antiques shop."

"Pippa, that whole tour is just a scam to get money. It's a bit of entertainment. You can't take the stories too seriously, and you can't let them impact a business decision."

"But the rumors have been around for way longer than the tour has been running!" Pippa caught my skeptical expression and lowered her voice. "You know that painting that's been sitting in the corner for years—the one of the young girl and boy."

I swallowed. I knew the one she meant. A large watercolor in a bronze frame of a pair of children, painted like they were in the 1940s, but cartoon like. Both children had been painted with large cartoon-like eyes that dwarfed their faces, and the eyes seemed to follow you. I always hurried past it, it gave me the creeps. The painting had been in the store, in the same place, in the front window, for as long as I could remember.

"What about it?" I picked up a cloth and began to wipe the tables, as though I wasn't really interested in what Pippa was saying, when actually I had my ears keenly pricked, waiting for her response.

"They say that painting is haunted. That's why it never sells. No one wants it in their home."

I stood up straight. "Well, that's the silliest thing I've ever heard." I shook my head. "That painting doesn't sell because it's over-priced. Not to mention ugly. Besides, the painting won't be there once I buy the store, none of the antiques will."

Pippa shook her head. "The rumors say that the boy

and girl live in the painting..."

"The boy and girl are painted onto the canvas," I corrected her.

Pippa ignored me. "The story goes that they live in the shop. They've lived there for decades. That's why the painting never sells. They don't let anyone buy it. They can't be moved from their home. Rachael, if you buy the shop and try to get rid of the painting, then the children will be very upset. They will curse you."

I stood there staring at Pippa like she had gone out of her mind. "Okay, Pippa, that's a great story. But unfortunately, some of us have to live in reality. Some of us have a business to run."

"Rachael, I am warning you. If you buy that shop, and try to get rid of the painting, you will pay the price!"

***

I told Pippa I needed to run to the post office so that she wouldn't try to stop me, but as soon as I was out the door, I went off in the opposite direction, towards the mortgage firm where I was meeting the landlord of the antiques shop--a tall, thin man named Bruce who had a pencil thin mustache and eyebrows that always looked raised.

He pushed the contract over to me and I gave it a look over. "That should all be in order."

Yes, I decided. *This is the right time to do it. Time to take the plunge.*

"Great," I said, smiling at him. "I'll give it to my lawyer to look over, and then sign it. I should have it back to you by tomorrow."

"Tomorrow?" he asked nervously, his raised eyebrows disappearing even further up into his forehead. "Why can't you sign them now? I can assure you everything is in order."

I stood up as a show of confidence. "I just need to make sure everything is in place. Tomorrow will be fine, won't it? Not much can change by tomorrow!"

As soon as I stepped out of the bank, the heavens opened and I stared up at the sky, mouth agape, to find the sky, which had been a bright blue before I'd stepped into the bank, was now practically black, filled with angry swirling clouds that spewed icy rain all over the streets.

And I didn't even have an umbrella with me.

Using my purse as a shield over my head, I raced back to the bakery, cursing the fact that I hadn't looked at the weather forecast.

"It wasn't predicted by the weather weather man," Pippa informed me warily as I shook myself off, causing a small puddle to form in the entryway of the shop. "Where have you been?" She stopped frothing the milk for the cappuccino she was making and looked me up and down.

"I told you, the post office."

"The way to the post office is totally covered. You've been the other way."

Sprung.

"Okay, fine," I said with a sigh, pulling the contract out of my bag to show her.

"Oh, Rachael..." Her face was grave. "Aren't you going to listen to anything I told you?"

"Pippa, it will be fine. I can't be put off by a silly superstition."

She handed the contract back to me and crossed her arms. "It's more than that, Rachael." She shivered and looked up at the ceiling. "You've set events in motion now by taking that contract."

"I haven't signed it yet," I pointed out. Not that I believed anything she was going on about.

"That doesn't matter, Rachael. It will already be starting."

I sighed and took off my soaking wet red peacoat and hung it on a hook by the door. As I stepped back towards the counter I heard a snapping sound and heard my heavy coat fall to the floor, the hook taking off a chunk of paint and plaster with it as it tumbled after the coat.

"It's just an old hook, Pippa," I said, staring at it. "And the coat was heavy from the rain."

"I'm telling you..."

There was a crashing sound and all of a sudden we were encased in darkness. Outside, the sky was so dark that without lights in the shop, there was no light at all.

Pippa let out a shriek and rubbed her arms as though she had the worst case of the chills the world had ever seen.

"It's just a blown fuse, Pippa," I said, catching the gleam of the whites of her eyes. I could tell what she was thinking before she even said it. "Or a power line has come down in the storm. Calm down, Pippa. Think rationally."

"It's the curse, Rachael. It's already started."

Chapter 2

Curses were just going to have to wait. As soon as I had confirmation from my lawyer that I wasn't getting ripped off, all it required was my signature.

My hand hovered above the blank line. It wasn't Pippa's curse getting in my head. It was a different kind of fear. Fear of the unknown. Fear of failing.

It hadn't been that long ago that I'd thought my bakery was going to go under. Could I really take a risk like this? What if disaster struck again?

What if there really was a curse?

I shook myself off. That was the dumbest fear of them all. Trying not to let my worries get a second look in, I scrawled my name across the dotted line.

"There!" I said proudly. "Done." Now it was just a matter of handing it in. "See," I said out loud as I grabbed my coat. "I knew nothing would happen between yesterday and today."

Pippa was still fast asleep on the sofa. She had enough money now to afford her own place, but she'd said she'd gotten into the habit of sleeping there and was in no hurry to hunt for apartments yet and my sofa was a great rent saver. Truthfully, I thought the stories from the paranormal club had gotten to her and she was too scared to live alone but didn't want to admit it. Anyway, I didn't mind her living with me, I only wished I had a second bedroom. I glanced down at the contract, hot in my hands. All my extra funds had to go into the business for the time being, not into a bigger apartment.

"Come on, Pips, I can't wait for you forever," I called out.

Pippa lifted her head off the sofa and pouted with her arms crossed over her chest. "Well, you're going to have to. I'm not coming. I can't be a part of this curse."

I stood there with my mouth wide open. "What do you mean you're not coming? Thanks for the support, Pip. This is kind of a big deal for me, you know. I was counting on my friend for moral support."

A look of guilt interrupted Pippa's pout. She tossed the covers off and stood up with a sigh. "Fine. I will come with you to hand over the papers. But if anything spooky or scary happens, I am out of there."

"Nothing spooky or scary is going to happen, Pippa. Come on."

***

I had spoken far too soon.

"What the heck is going on down there?" Pippa stopped short in the middle of the street while I stood next to her, shivering and wanting to get a move on. There was a definite winter's chill in the air and I was keen to get indoors.

"Don't get distracted, Pippa. We've got to get to the antique shop."

Pippa pointed. "That's where all the fuss is, Rach. Look."

I stopped and looked towards where she pointed. In front of the antiques shop was a bunch of police vans, and the entire store had been taped off with police tape.

"What the..." I murmured. I began to hurry towards the shop, but Pippa grabbed my sleeve and pulled me back.

Please just let it be a break-in, I thought.

"Rach, I told you, if anything scary happens..."

"Pippa, I'm about to be the owner of that shop that is surrounded by police! I need to find out what is

16

happening." I broke free of her grip and hurried towards the scene where I saw a familiar face.

"Detective Whitaker," I said, coming to a stop.

Uh-oh. If he was here, that meant it was serious. It was unlikely to be just a simple robbery.

It seemed to take him a few moments to register who I was. I tried not to take it personally.

"Rachael," he said as he stopped whatever he was writing on his notepad.

"Jackson, what's happening?" My voice came out far more vexed and breathless than I'd intended it to. I tried to push past, craning my neck to get a better look at what was happening inside the shop, but Jackson stopped me.

"This is police business, Rachael. You can't get back there."

"But I'm the owner of the store. At least, I'm about to be." He frowned so I pulled the contract out of my coat pocket and waved it around in his face, as though the act might grant me access to the crime scene.

"But you're not the owner now?" Jackson looked very serious.

"Well, no," I said helplessly. "But I'm buying this

shop. Please, you need to tell me what is going on. I need to know if I've made a huge mistake." I looked up at him and made my best damsel-in-distress face. "Please, Jackson," I whispered. "As a friend."

I wasn't sure that's what we were, exactly, but he looked left and right at the crowd and then nodded at me slightly.

"There's been a body found inside," he said quietly, not quite looking at me as he spoke. He glanced all around him to make sure that no one overheard us. "A young man by the looks of it."

"A body?" My heart froze and I could feel a hard lump in my throat.

Not again.

"Like...a dead body?" I whispered.

I saw the look on Jackson's face. Okay, dumb question. But I couldn't believe what I had just heard. I leaned over and grabbed onto the police tape, which did little to steady me and I almost ended up face first on the concrete.

"Whoa there," Jackson said, reaching out for me. A few people in the crowd tittered amongst each other at the sight of my almost fainting.

"Come with me," Jackson said, leading me to the back of a police van. I could feel everyone's eyes on me and I was vaguely aware that this made me look like I was guilty, but my legs were so unsteady and my head was swimming so fast that I didn't care. I just needed to sit down.

Jackson wrapped a blanket around me and offered me a Styrofoam cup filled with water. I took it with shaking hands and tried to take a sip.

"I'm sorry. I'm so embarrassed..." I said once the ringing in my ears had stopped. "I don't even know what came over me. I'm just...shocked. That's all."

Jackson shot me a small smile and a sympathetic look. "Seems like a lot of this sort of thing is happening around here lately."

I stopped sipping my water. "A lot of what, exactly?" I asked cautiously.

Jackson shrugged. "Murder."

My heart clenched up again. "Murder?" I whispered. "So that body you found...it wasn't an accident?"

I saw a look of dismay take over Jackson's face and a faint blush crept up his cheeks. "I...I shouldn't have said that." He coughed. "The details are not clear yet. We're still investigating."

"But you think it's a murder."

"Rach, I didn't..."

"Detective Whitaker," a stern female voice called out. "We need you back inside."

Jackson shot me an apologetic look and promised to check on me later. He made me promise to wait there a while and rest. But as soon as he was out of eyeshot, I stood up and threw my cup in the trash.

"Pippa," I called out breathlessly, running back to where she still stood, seemingly frozen in shock. "Pippa, someone was murdered in the antiques shop."

She turned to me slowly. "Now are you going to believe me, Rachael?"

"Believe you about what?" It took a moment or two for me to figure out what she was going on about. "Pippa, you have to be kidding me..."

Her voice was low and foreboding. "I told you, Rach. The children in the painting. They won't let their home be taken from them."

I placed my hands on my hips. "So what are you saying, Pippa? That the children in the painting have *killed* someone? Seriously, just think for a second about how ridiculous that sounds..."

Pippa gave me a long, low look. "I've already warned you twice, Rachael. First the storm, then the hook coming off the wall--on the side of the bakery that is next door to the antiques shop even!"

I rolled my eyes.

"Then the blackout that was confined to our building."

I shifted from one foot to the other. Now that one was a little harder to explain away. We'd checked the fuse box and it had been fine. And no other buildings on the street had been affected. The lights had mysteriously come back on three hours later, but by then, we'd already lost all our preparation time for the following day, costing me a great deal of time and money. Still, there had to be a logical explanation.

Didn't there?

Pippa was still standing with her hands on her hips.

"Now the twins are sending you an even more serious warning. Are you really going to buy that shop, Rachael? Are you really going to work in there? Run your business from that place?"

I stared up ahead as a stretcher with a body bag

lying on top was pushed from the shop into a waiting ambulance.

I gulped and reached into my pocket to feel the contract still waiting to be handed over.

If I was still going to buy the shop, I was going to have to figure out who killed that young man.

Pippa was still staring at the shop. She was so blue and pale that she was practically translucent. Her eyes were glazed over, but there was a distinct look of fear frozen inside them.

And I realized: more than anything else, I was going to have to prove that the killer was human.

Chapter 3

I leaned over and inspected the rows of flaky pastry topped with thick, hard vanilla frosting. My personal favorite: Vanilla Slice.

But not my personal recipe.

Pippa held her breath. "Well?" she finally squeaked. "What's the verdict?"

"Hmm, they smell good, but I think I'm going to have to sample one just to make sure." Pippa almost turned blue as she waited for me to sample the dessert. The pastry was perfectly crisp and flaky, and the custard was soft but firm without being gelatinous.

I narrowed my eyes at her as I leaned against the counter, stringing out my verdict like I was the judge on a reality show.

"I give them a nine out of ten."

Pippa heaved a sigh of relief. "Thank goodness. I was so worried that Romeo wouldn't be up to the job. Oh, I'm so glad you like them, Rach."

Romeo was Pippa's first hire in her role as assistant manager. One of the perks of expanding was that I could hire an apprentice baker, and one of the other perks was that I could outsource some of my managerial duties. I'd been a little nervous leaving Pippa in charge of hiring, but not as nervous as she had been about finding the right person. Romeo was a talented baker, even though he could be a little grumpy, but that could have just been due to the early hours that bakers had to keep. I could cut him a little slack on that. Been there, done that. I was grateful that I occasionally got to sleep in these days.

Speak of the devil, Romeo trudged out of the kitchen, wiping his flour-covered hands on his apron as he scowled at the two of us. His dark curly hair was sticking out from underneath his cap and I could tell from the bags hanging under his eyes that the 3:00 A.M. alarms were already taking their toll on him.

"Good morning," I said, smiling brightly at him.

"I need coffee," he said back, heading straight for our espresso machine. I placed my hand gently in front of the machine, stopping him.

"You don't need to do that. How about I run and get coffee for all of us from that new place down the road, the Red Ribbon, I think it's called, as a treat?" I asked cheerily. "They've got some amazing flavors..."

Pippa nodded eagerly and told me she'd take a cookies and cream iced coffee. Romeo was still scowling but he reluctantly said he'd take a short black. "You sure you don't want anything a bit special?"

"Short black," he said gruffly.

Pippa and I looked at each other as he stomped back to the kitchen and we both burst into laughter as the door swung shut behind him. "He's only twenty but he acts like a grumpy old man."

Pippa agreed. "Sorry that he's so...tempestuous, though. I swear, at the interview he was a lot more friendly."

"You don't need to apologize for his every action, Pippa. You can't be held responsible for his attitude. Besides, as long as he keeps baking like this, he can give me all the attitude he likes...just don't tell him that," I added, before I grabbed my purse to head out the door. "I'll be back in ten!"

***

There was a long line at the Red Ribbon when I arrived. Maybe I was going to be little longer than ten minutes. I glanced over my shoulder at the bakery, wondering if Romeo could go that long without his coffee before he started murdering people.

Poor choice of words.

"Hey!" a voice called and I jumped. "You look like you're a million miles away there."

"Jackson...Detective, I mean," I said, straightening up. "Just hoping that everyone at the bakery is okay without me." Not thinking about murder.

He grinned at me. "I'm sure they'll manage just fine without you. Why don't you sit down and join me for a little while?"

I really shouldn't.

But I did have an ulterior motive for wanting to chat with Jackson, and it wasn't just to sit down and take a break. I was hoping that he might let some details of the case slip out if I could get him to relax a little. I couldn't just come straight out and ask him for police information, but over coffee, I might be able to get something out of him.

But I kept thinking about Pippa being stuck on her own with Romeo on a rampage.

Jackson seemed to sense my hesitation. "Come on,

I'll even buy your coffee."

He placed our order and I ordered Romeo and Pippa's to-go in half an hour.

I settled into a booth. "I'll just tell them the line was long. Really, really long."

"You don't have to feel guilty for taking a few minutes to yourself, Rachael," Jackson said as he slipped into the seat across from me. "You've worked non-stop the last few years to get that bakery to the point where it can take care of itself."

"It's not that," I said, stirring even more sugar into my vanilla latte. Romeo wasn't the only person that morning who needed a pick-me-up, but I relied on sugar over caffeine for my morning hit.

I chose my next words carefully. "I'm just a little on edge after everything that happened yesterday."

Jackson sat his coffee mug down. "Right," he murmured. "That would be a huge thing for you right now. Has business been affected?"

I shook my head. "Not like last time." Last time someone had been murdered on this street, I'd almost gone of out business. But last time the murder weapon had been a pie. This time it had been...that was just one detail I needed to get from Jackson.

I waited for Jackson's reaction. "The last time. Right. Trouble sure does seem to be following you lately."

"So how was the man killed?" I interrupted him, speaking far more bluntly than I'd intended. *Great, Rach,* I scolded myself. *Way to be subtle about getting info.*

He narrowed his eyes at me. "We don't know that yet." He picked up his mug again and took a sip, watching me closely. "Do you?"

"Of course not," I replied quickly. "How would I know that?"

He shrugged. "Like I said, trouble seems to be following you lately."

"Pippa has this crazy idea that I am being haunted," I said, rolling my eyes.

I expected Jackson to laugh, but instead he just gave me a long look. "Weird things do seem to happen around you, Rachael." Now he looked suspicious. "Things like people getting killed."

I was outraged. "Are you suggesting I might have been in some way responsible for that guy's death?" We'd been down this road before. Last time a person had died on this street, I'd been a prime suspect in her murder, until I'd been able to solve it and clear my own name.

Jackson sighed. "I would have already brought you in for questioning if you were. Don't worry, you'll know about it if you become a suspect."

That was reassuring. "I have an alibi you know. I was with Pippa all night." This wasn't exactly how I'd wanted the conversation to go. I'd wanted to get information from him, not become a suspect.

He told me to take a breath, relax. Which was easier said than done.

It wasn't that I believed Pippa's haunted house stories. But Jackson was right: death seemed to be following me.

I shivered.

"Here, I'll order you another coffee."

I shook my head. "I need to go," I said, standing up abruptly. Jackson looked disappointed. "Sorry, there's just something I need to do."

***

"Shoot," I said, stepping through the door as I realized I'd forgotten Pippa and Romeo's coffees.

"Where have you been?" Pippa asked. "You've been gone for over half an hour."

"The line was massive." I threw my empty hands up into the air. "So I just gave up. I hope Romeo isn't going to kill me."

Pippa sighed and crossed her arms, glancing back over her shoulder at the kitchen with a worried look on her face. "Well, I think Romeo's coffee is the least of your problems right now."

"What do you mean?" I heard a crashing sound and then the back door slamming shut. "Pippa," I shouted, running towards the kitchen. "Is that the sound of Romeo leaving? What's going on here?"

She chased after me as I opened the door to find a kitchen in absolute chaos. There were overturned bowls everywhere, flour and pastry and cake mix covering every surface, including the walls and floor. "Has something exploded in here?" I asked Pippa.

"Yeah," she answered. "Romeo."

My jaw was open wide. "I've heard of people getting grumpy because they don't get their morning coffee, but this is just insane. Pippa, what happened?"

I turned to find her huddled against the door looking guilty. "I don't know, Rach, but I think whatever was upsetting him, it was something more serious than coffee. I don't think he got any sleep last night. He was in a rotten mood all morning. I mean, he's always a bit surly but today it was on another level."

I looked at the mess all around me in horror. "Well, is he coming back?"

Pippa threw her hands in the air. "I'm sorry, Rach. I don't know." She hung her head. "This is my fault. I should never have hired him."

I turned to leave. "Just try and get him back, by this afternoon preferably. Otherwise, we're going to have to find another apprentice baker. Or have nothing to serve this afternoon."

***

"It's the curse," Pippa said as our meager supply of cakes ran out shortly after lunchtime.

"What is?" I asked.

Pippa shrugged and looked down at the empty display cases. "This," she said, pointing to them.

I turned towards her slowly. "Are you trying to blame Romeo's unprofessionalism on a *curse?* I'm pretty sure that was all just due to him being a bad employee. And young. Not everyone can handle the stress of the early hours. There's nothing paranormal about it. In fact, it's very normal to react badly to poor sleep."

Pippa shook her head. "I told you, the twins will do everything they can to stay in their home." She grabbed me by the shoulders. "And they will do everything they can to stop you from taking over. Screwing with your staff, and your cash supply, so that you can't buy the store!"

"I am buying the store. One poor day of sales can't stop me."

Pippa turned white. "You're really going to ignore all this?" she whispered.

I had to turn the sign on the door to "closed," seeing as we had nothing to serve for the rest to the afternoon.

"Should I place another job ad?" Pippa asked quietly.

"Not just yet. Let's see if Romeo comes back." Even though he had acted atrociously, I was willing to give him another chance, based on his age and baking skills, and also largely due to the fact that we'd all been through a bit of a shock following the previous day's events.

"I can wait, Rachael, but I don't think Romeo is coming back. He's as freaked out as I am."

I stopped and stared at her. "What does that mean?"

"Nothing," she said quickly, picking up a broom. "Just that he was on edge."

"Does he believe this crazy story as well? Did you put these ideas in his head?" I took a step towards her. "Come on, Pippa, you better tell me what really happened this morning in the kitchen."

"Nothing," she repeated. "I don't know what was up with Romeo today. He just went crazy." She swept a bit of rubbish into a pile and brushed the stack into the bin. "But I wouldn't blame him if he was too scared to keep working here."

"Fine, Pippa. If you're so hell-bent on sticking to your crazy haunted painting theory, then come with me to the antiques shop and prove it to me."

Pippa's eyes were so wide that all I could see were the whites. With her bright blue hair, she looked a little bit like a circus clown. "Fine," she finally said. "But if anything happens while we're snooping around, you have to take it as your final warning. To stay away from the place. Deal?"

I hesitated. But what were the chances of something odd happening? "Deal," I agreed.

Chapter 4

It was 1:00 A.M. I'd been out on the back of the street at this time before, but that was only once when I had a mountain of pastries to bake and no staff to help me.

"Actually, after we finish this snooping around, I will probably have to start work," I grumbled. "On zero sleep. You thought Romeo was bad today. I'm going to be a match for him." I paused. "You haven't heard from him by any chance, have you?"

Pippa shook her head. As she spoke, the chill in the air caused her words to steam in front of her. "I'll find an even better baker for you, Rach, I promise. I'll make it up to you."

"Don't worry about that now," I said gently. "Let's just concentrate on what we're doing here."

Pippa shocked me when, instead of heading towards the back entrance of the antiques shop, she started walking around the front.

"Where are you going?" I called out in a shout that I tried to keep to a whisper.

She stopped for a moment. "The back is deadbolted,

I can't pick that. The front is just a regular lock."

I ran after her. The streetlights at the front of the shop suddenly cast a sobering light on what we were doing.

"We really shouldn't be going inside," I said, glancing at the yellow tape that still surrounded the antiques shop. "We could be arrested for tampering with a crime scene."

"It was your idea." Pippa pushed past me and began to search around with a flashlight.

I pushed the flashlight down and told her to keep quiet. "Someone will see us."

"Well, how are *we* supposed to see?" Pippa shivered. "I'm not going inside that place without any light."

"Fine."

We crept up to the door and Pippa took a pin out of her hair. I'd heard the rumors about her prowess with lock-picking, but I'd never actually seen her skills first hand.

"Keep a look out, Rach." She didn't need to tell me twice. Last thing I wanted was to get arrested for breaking and entering. Detective Whitaker would put me at the top of his suspects list for the guy's murder.

I told myself that we weren't there to cause any damage, or to even touch anything. We were there to help solve a crime. That helped ease my guilty conscious a little bit.

"What would I do without you, Pips?" I had to admire the way she'd picked the lock like a skilled pro. Although, as I stepped over the threshold and glanced at the popped lock, I couldn't help but think about the fact that I would have had the keys by now, if the slight problem of the murder hadn't taken place.

Pippa was stalking ahead with a confidence that surprised me. After all her stories, I'd been expecting her to cower behind me. "Wait up," I called, as she had the flashlight and it was difficult for me to see three paces behind her.

I coughed as soon as the heavy dust hit my nostrils and settled there. "I'm gonna have to give this place a good scrubbing before I actually serve food here."

"You're going to have to give it more than a good scrubbing," Pippa muttered. "I'm thinking more like an exorcism."

She shone the flashlight on item after item. Old paintings, vases, statues, trunks, furniture and more flickered into view before going dark again.

"I've never actually been inside this place before. There's so much junk." I moved around carefully, trying not to knock any of the tall vases lest they smash and give us away to anyone still awake and nearby. "I wonder where Gus is going to store all this stuff once he goes out of business."

"Probably in the garbage," Pippa said, then she stopped. She had the flashlight trained on...*it.*

"I can't believe this is still in here," Pippa whispered as she stared at the old fashioned painting. The twin boy and girl depicted in it, both around three years of age, stared eerily back at her.

"Well, where did you think it would be? Taken down to the station for questioning?" My joke was an attempt at easing the fear emanating from her, but Pippa just stared back at the painting, the flashlight trembling in her hand.

"What, Pippa? What is it?"

"Rachael, it's...it's moving..."

I stared straight into the eyes of the girl and boy depicted in the picture, almost expecting their eyes to be moving, for the picture to come to life.

Pippa really was getting to me. I shook my head and

closed my eyes. "Pippa, paintings can't move."

She looked at me like I was crazy. Then I saw what she meant. It wasn't the figures in the painting that were moving (okay, I have to admit that was a little insane) but the entire frame. It was shaking and moving from side to side.

Despite my better senses, I screamed and almost pushed Pippa over in my rush to get out of the shop. Still shrieking, I pulled frantically on the door, screaming for it to open before Pippa came up behind me and pointed out that I needed to push it.

We both spilled out onto the street, doubled over as we struggled to catch our breaths. I felt like there were razor blades in my lungs. And like my heart had been electrocuted.

"What the heck was that?" I finally asked. I could hear the trembling in my voice. I looked down to see that my hands were shaking. "Why the heck was it moving?"

I looked over at Pippa and noticed that she was empty handed. "Pippa! You dropped the flashlight in there!"

Pippa was shaking even harder than I was. "So?" she asked. "Let's scooch! We need to get away from this place before whatever is in there gets us." She was like a wild animal, up on her hind legs ready to flee.

I steadied my breathing. One of us had to keep our cool. "I agree that we need to get away from this place, but we can't leave the flashlight in there. Someone will figure out it's ours. "

Pippa shook her head frantically. "There's no way they'll know it belonged to us."

"Your fingerprints are all over it, Pippa."

"I don't care."

"We need to go back in there and get it."

Pippa just stared at me and backed away from the door. "Well, you'll have to go back in on your own."

"Pippa..."

I stared inside the shop in dismay. Total blackness. The thought of stepping back in there, with that thing moving around sent shivers up my spine.

"Well?" Pippa said. Even with the fear present in her voice, I could hear the tone of triumph shining through. "Are you really going back in there alone, Rach?"

I slowly turned back to her, shaking my head. "No."

***

I didn't get much sleep that night. And it wasn't just due to the fact I had to be up at 5:00 A.M. thanks to Romeo's sudden disappearance. Every time I shut my eyes, all I could see was that painting, rocking back and forth, taunting me. Heck, maybe those painted eyes really were moving!

"Hey," Pippa called out as I shuffled into the kitchen. I jumped a mile.

"Sorry, I didn't mean to scare you." Pippa dug a spoon into her bowl of cereal while she sat at the bench.

I tried to play off my nerves. "I'm just startled to see you up this early, that's all. You usually don't rise until well past midday if you can help it."

"I couldn't sleep either," she replied softly.

"Who says I didn't sleep?" I didn't know why I was so intent on proving to Pippa that I wasn't rattled. I just didn't want to admit that what happened the night before had actually happened. But there was no explanation for it. And that made me uncomfortable for more than one reason.

Pippa gave me a long, slow look before she jumped

up to rinse her bowl. "Well, I've got a plan," she announced. I popped a slice of bread in the toaster and waited. "I'm going to call an emergency meeting of the Belldale Paranormal Society."

"That's your plan?"

"Rachael, they'll know what's going on. They'll have answers."

I rolled my eyes. "Pippa, I really think you ought to stop hanging around with the people in that club. They are seriously messing with your mind, and now the craziness is rubbing off on other people." I reached for a carton of juice and slammed the refrigerator shut. The only reason I'd been freaked out so much the night before was because of Pippa's outlandish claims.

Pippa pouted. "So you think I've gone crazy?"

I looked at Pippa with her frizzy blue hair sticking out at crazy angles. I'd always thought she was a little crazy. But in a good way.

I smiled at her. "What do you mean 'gone crazy'? I think you're already there."

She gave me a playful push, then turned somber. "I know some of their ideas are a little wacky when you hear them for the first time, but if you'd just come along for a meeting..."

"Pippa, there's no way I'm coming to a meeting."

She looked hurt. "Why not?"

I didn't know. A hundred reasons. Too busy running a successful business, too concerned with logic...

Pippa tilted her head to the side when I didn't immediately answer. "Are you scared?" Her tone was teasing. And I wasn't about to fall for that tactic.

I sighed. "No, I'm not scared."

"Because some of them are witches," Pippa said with a bit of awe in her voice. I was glad my head was facing towards the refrigerator, as she would have taken even further offense if she could see the face I made. "But don't worry, if I say that you're with me, they won't do any harm to you."

That was the last worry I had. My primary worry was that I would lose my respected reputation if I was seen entering or exiting a meeting of the Belldale Paranormal Society.

"Please, Rach, at least think about it."

I was about to tell her that there was no way I was even going to think about it when we both heard something crash in the hallway. We jumped like startled cats and I could feel all my hair on edge as I crept into the hall to see what had made that insanely loud noise.

It was still dark outside and the hallway was black. I fumbled until I found the light switch and gasped when I stepped back and banged into Pippa.

"Sorry," she whispered.

Suddenly there was light and the whole thing didn't seem quite so scary, but then I saw what the noise was. There was a picture frame lying in the middle of the hall, smashed into a thousand different bits, with glass scattered everywhere.

My first thought was, *how in the heck am I going to have time to clean all that up before I start work?*

But Pippa was trembling as she approached it. "Rach... Look what this is a picture of..."

I had to follow her to see what she was talking about. My walls are lined with dozens of random photos and paintings. If you'd asked me before then to tell you what artwork was in a specific part of the house, I wouldn't be able to tell you. "What is it a picture of?"

Pippa seemed to know my own decor better than I did. She pointed at the smashed frame to the corner of the picture. At first glance, the picture was nothing more than a landscape, an oil color of an old fashioned scene, a golden field with an old house in the background and a bridge in the front of the house.

But in the corner... In the corner, so tiny you could hardly see them, were two tiny little children.

They looked about four years old. They looked like twins.

I looked at Pippa. Maybe a meeting of the Belldale Paranormal Society wouldn't be such a bad idea after all.

Chapter 5

Knock, knock.

A girl—woman—possibly in her late teens or early twenties stood there. She had long dyed purplish-red hair and pale porcelain skin. She was wearing a cape that made her look like Red Riding Hood, except that she was dressed in black.

"Is Pippa here?" she said in a tone so quiet I had to lean forward to be able to hear her.

I suddenly knew who she was. Or, at least, where she was from. The Belldale Paranormal club.

I shook my head. "She's at work." Pippa was covering for me because I was feeling quite ill with a headache and fever. Three days had passed since the incident with the painting in the hallway and—so far—nothing else unusual had happened.

Of course, Pippa was blaming my illness on the so-called 'curse.' Another sign that the twins would do anything to keep me from buying the antiques shop.

But I had another reason for wanting to take a little time away from the bakery. I just couldn't accept Pippa's explanation of events. There had to be a logical explanation for everything that had happened, so I had decided to use my sick day for something more than just lying on the sofa and watching Criminal Point: I was going to get to the bottom of everything.

I wasn't too impressed with the woman in front of me and certainly didn't want to waste my time on her. Hoping to end the interaction quickly, I started to close the door but she stepped in front of it.

"Maybe I should talk to you then."

I didn't really like the sound of that. "I'm a little busy right now," I said politely. "Fighting off a bit of the flu, actually. I wouldn't want you to get infected."

"Oh, I won't get infected," she said with eyes that opened so wide it was a little creepy. "I have a spell that makes me immune from all the winter bugs."

Oh boy.

"I can cast it on you if you like?"

"No, thanks. I've got plenty of aspirin and throat lozenges. Those are my magical spells."

She didn't seem amused. Her face had a ghostly, otherworldly quality. "Are you Rachael? Pippa's told me a lot about you."

I nodded. "The one and only."

"I'm Tegan," she replied.

The name was familiar to me. I now knew exactly who she was. She was the leader of the Belldale Paranormal Society. The one that called all the shots.

Most likely the one that had put all the crazy ideas into Pippa's head in the first place. I eyed her with suspicion.

"I really ought to go back inside. I'm feeling rather faint."

Tegan eyed me like she could see right through me. Literally. But also as though she could tell that I was lying. "Rachael, Pippa told me about all the mysterious things that have been happening to you."

"Did she?" I asked heavily.

Tegan nodded. "It sounds to me like you have had a curse placed on you, Rachael."

"Don't be ridiculous." I tried to close the door again.

She stopped me. "I can help you, Rachael, if you let me. I know what's going on."

She peered at me again with those eyes that seemed to see directly into my soul.

I gulped and shook my head. "I don't need your help,

thank you."

***

One little peek through the window couldn't hurt.

I leaned close to the window, cupping my hands around my face to get a better look. Suddenly, a figure started lunging towards me and I screamed. Pulling back, my breathing returned to something resembling normal when I saw it was the antique store's owner, Gus.

Gus was in his late fifties and always seemed a little gruff, his clothes were always as dusty as the antiques he kept in his shop. I'd seen less and less of him over the last few months as he'd been ill and mostly leaving the shop in the hands of his family. To tell the truth, I was glad I hadn't had much interaction with him, given that I was in the process of buying his store—effectively pushing him out of business.

"Gus!" I said, plastering a smile on my face as he opened the door for me. This was a little awkward. Even though my intended purchase of his store was nothing personal, he probably still resented me for the fact that I would be its new owner.

"Hello, Rachael." We'd always been on friendly terms since I'd opened the bakery three years earlier and I was relieved to find that he didn't seem, on the surface at least, to harbor any ill will towards me.

"Is everything okay?" I asked him. Stupid question. Of course it wasn't. Not only was the poor guy about to sell the business he had put his blood, sweat and tears into, there was now the problem of the shop being...well, literally filled with blood, sweat, and tears.

"Besides the fact that a man was murdered in my shop..." Gus started, and I braced myself. His forehead creased into a deep frown. "There was a break-in a few days ago."

I froze.

"A break-in?" I asked, trying to keep my voice steady.

"Some stuff was moved around. And they were stupid enough to leave a flashlight in here."

Yes, they were.

"Oh no," I said, pretending to be outraged. "That's terrible, Gus. Do you know who it was?"

Gus shook his head. "No. And strange as it is, it

seems like they didn't take anything. But it makes you wonder, doesn't it?"

"It does."

"Whoever it was that killed that poor guy, they might have come back to clean up after themselves."

"Well, if they left a flashlight behind, they mustn't have done a very good job of cleaning up!" I let out a forced high-pitched laugh that was far too loud.

He gave me a suspicious look. "You didn't happen so see anything that night, did you?"

I shook my head quickly. "No, I was home in bed early that night."

He narrowed his eyes. "I didn't tell you exactly what night it was yet."

I gulped and checked the time on my phone. "Shoot, Gus, I really gotta go. We're down a baker at the store and I've been doing double duty." That wasn't exactly true. If anyone had been pulling double duty, it was Pippa. But I had to get out of there.

But I stopped just as I reached the door. I could hear the rush of customers on the other side and even through the cracks, I could smell cinnamon and vanilla wafting out. And there was Gus next to me, dutifully, sadly, clearing out the remains of a dying shop—a shop that was a crime scene no less. I wondered if hearing my own full shop next to him was just like the final twist of the knife in his guts.

I snuck in and grabbed a Danish pastry without anyone noticing me. Pippa was running around and wouldn't have noticed if the president walked in at that moment. I couldn't do much to help Gus, but I could do one thing: offer him pastry.

I tiptoed back to Gus's shop, hoping to surprise him, but I stopped short at the door when I saw what Gus was doing. I made sure no one was looking before I pressed my face closer to the glass. He was tampering with the painting of the twins. I looked closer. It looked like he was pulling wire off the top of the frame.

Wire that could have easily been used to move the painting from side-to-side. Wire that could have been used to scare off trespassers.

Gus suddenly looked up at me, locking eyes on me like I was a target. I dropped the Danish pastry and backed away from the window, but he was already storming towards the door.

"What are you doing?" he growled. Then, with a small satisfied scoff, "Snooping around again, I see."

"Again?"

"I know it was you and your friend here the other night."

I steadied my breathing. "Oh yeah? How could you know that unless you were here as well?" I raised an eyebrow at him, daring him to come up with a good answer for that.

His lips moved silently for a moment. I'd got him. It must have been him in the shop that night, moving the painting around and trying to scare us off.

But why?

When he didn't answer, I backed away and left the pastry lying there on the ground, waiting for the stray cats to come and get it after dark.

***

"Pippa," I said, grabbing her as I ran into the bakery. "I've got to tell you something! It's urgent. I've had a major breakthrough in the case."

She opened her mouth in disbelief.

"Rachael, we're slammed right now, can't you see

that?" She pointed to the long line of customers snaking out the door. "You could lend a hand if you wanted," she said, a little too pointedly.

I nodded. "Sorry," I said, grabbing an apron. As we rushed to serve customers, I managed to whisper a few details to her, but it wasn't until we closed that I was finally able to tell her the information that was about to burst out of me.

"Pippa," I said, taking my apron off. "Listen to this." I waited until I had her full attention. "I think Gus is the one who killed that person in the antiques shop!"

Pippa frowned as she placed a tray of brownies back in the fridge. The sweet smell made my tummy rumble and I stopped the door before it shut, grabbing one and taking a bite of the heavenly brownie. "Boy, I was starving. Especially after the day I've had."

"Me too," Pippa said. "I didn't get a chance to take a lunch break." Again, her tone was rather pointed.

"Are you mad at me Pippa?"

"I just think..." She slammed the door of the fridge shut. "That you've been spending so much time on this investigation that you're neglecting your duties here. And I'm the one whose been left to pick up all the slack."

I placed my brownie on the counter. "You're the one who keeps telling me that there is a mystery to solve, Pippa."

"No. I keep telling you to stay out of it."

"So that's what all this is about? You're so scared of all this silly superstition that you want me to drop it? What are you so worried is going to happen to you, Pippa?"

"Rach," she whispered, "I'm worried that something really bad is going to happen to *you.*"

She didn't sound so worried about me right then. Sounded like she was more worried about being overworked. But I didn't want to say that. "Pippa, I really appreciate you helping me out. You know that, don't you?" We were getting well off track now. This was not how I'd imagined the conversation going in my head.

She nodded. "And I appreciate that you gave me this opportunity, Rach. I feel so bad about what happened with Romeo and I want to make it up to you. Sorry if I complained about feeling overworked."

"No, I'm sorry, Pips. How about I let you have tomorrow off and I cover both shifts?"

"But we still haven't gotten anyone to replace Romeo."

"Don't worry about it, I'll be fine. You take the day off and hang out with your friends from the paranormal society, if you like." I thought about telling Pippa about my run-in with Tegan earlier, but something about the whole interaction had creeped me out. I didn't really want her coming back to the house, but I figured bringing it up at all would only cause another potential argument.

I suggested we take a break. A proper one. "You need to eat, Pips. Anything you want is on the house."

***

"Okay, so tell me your theory about Gus then." Pippa had chosen to have a donut and a chocolate shake for her 'dinner,' which was fine by me. Though I couldn't help but think that it wouldn't hurt us to eat some vegetables one of these days. "Why do you think he did it?"

"Well, think about it, Pippa. He is the one with the most to lose out of the whole sale of the antiques store, isn't he?"

Pippa nodded and took a sip of her shake. "That's true."

I leaned in closer. "So what if he made up all these stories about the painting to try and scare off potential buyers. What if he even *killed* to keep potential buyers away?"

"I dunno, Rach. I don't think Gus was the originator of that story about the painting. That story has been around for years, and why would he make that up about his own shop while he was still trying to make money from it? Presumably, he wanted to sell that painting at some stage. The rumors would have done nothing to help him."

I was silent for a moment. Pippa was right. It was unlikely that Gus had invented the story. "There's still something that isn't right, Pippa. You should have seen the way he was acting before."

"Well, this must be a tough time for him."

Again, true.

"This isn't Scooby Doo, Rachael. Gus isn't pretending to be a ghost to try and drive potential buyers away. He's a middle-aged man. I'm sure he has a little more dignity than that. And I'm sure he could have come up with a better plan."

"Then what was he doing fooling around with that painting earlier? It definitely had some kind of wires hanging off of it. I didn't see enough before he caught me, but it looked like he was trying to remove them."

Pippa gave me a slow look. "Do we need to go back in there? Check it out? Maybe tonight after dark."

I picked up my latte and took a sip to buy me a little time. I knew, logically, that I wasn't cursed. I also knew, logically, that the antiques shop wasn't haunted. And I knew, more than likely, that it had been Gus screwing around with the painting that night.

So why was I still scared to go in there after dark? "I dunno, Pippa," I said when I finally gave an answer. "Gus already thinks we were snooping around the other night. If we get caught red-handed, it's not going to look good."

Pippa narrowed her eyes. "Are you sure that's all it is, Rachael? You're looking a little pale there."

"Just need to get some fruit and vegtables into my diet," I said quickly. "Still can't quite kick that flu from last week. I can't survive on brownies indefinitely by the looks of it. I just think we ought to back off sneaking around the antiques shop for a day or two."

Pippa shrugged and picked up her garbage to throw in the trash. I sat there for a moment trying to collect my thoughts while Pippa cleaned up. Once she'd taken the trash out back, I sighed and stood up to lock the front door. The sun had long disappeared from the sky and the street looked particularly eerie that night. I looked over my shoulder. I couldn't wait for Pippa to come back inside. Quickly, I grabbed my keys and locked the front door, pulling on it three times to make sure it was locked properly.

That's when I froze. There, standing on the other side of the street, staring straight through the window and into my soul, was Tegan.

Chapter 6

My cold seemed to be getting worse. I woke up with eyes so puffy that I could hardly see out of them and an awful pain in my gut.

"Rach, you look freaking terrible."

"Thanks," I said, pouring hot water over a peppermint tea bag. The smell was immediately soothing, even though I winced when I took a sip. The flavor always reminded me of being sick, as it's what my mom always used to give us kids when we had a flu or an upset stomach.

"I'm serious. You have to stay home." Pippa began to pull on her jacket, but I told her to take it off.

"It's okay, Pippa. I promised you the day off and I am going to stick to my promise. I'll be fine once I get there and the adrenaline sets in." I was actually hoping I'd be so rushed off my feet that I wouldn't have time to think about how rotten I felt.

Pippa pulled a face of semi-horror as she stared up at me. "Rach, you really don't look well enough to go to work. I'm worried about you."

"I'll be fine," I tried to reassure her, cringing at the

crackling in my voice. "It's just like I said: I need some more fresh fruit and veggies in my diet. I promise I won't snack on cakes and cookies all day."

But when I got to the bakery, those were about the only things I could stomach. As I forced a slice of brownie down, hoping to get my sugar hit to kick me into gear, I felt even worse.

What's happening to me? Doubled over, I clutched my stomach, wondering if I should go back on my word and ask Pippa to come in to cover me.

But then the morning rush began and I was right. I didn't even have time to think, let alone focus on my puffy face and labored breathing. And I managed to get through the day without throwing up.

But there was a downside to running around all day with no backup. I hadn't been able to clean as I went, and I was left standing in the middle of what looked like the wreckage of a tornado at the end of the day.

I grabbed a broom and mop and got to work. Now that I had time to think, all I could focus on was the aching in my limbs and the pulsing in my head.

The bakery's phone began to ring in a shrill pitch, cutting right into my headache. I limped over to it and picked up the receiver. "Hello?"

"Rach, it's me. You weren't picking up your cell."

"Battery's dead. Didn't have time to charge it. What's up, Pippa?"

"Are you going to be home soon?"

I glanced at the mess and chaos surrounding me. "Not for a few hours."

There was heaving breathing on the other end of the line. When she didn't reply, I asked if she was okay.

"I just don't like being all alone in the house after dark."

I glanced out the window. The days were getting shorter and shorter. 5:00 P.M. and the streets were completely dark. "I'll be home as soon as I can. You'll be fine though, Pippa. What do you think is going to happen to you?"

"Please, Rach, I'm really frightened."

"I've got a mountain of a mess to clean up. If I leave it like this, there'll be ants by morning, maybe even rats if we're really unlucky." I was growing a little impatient with Pippa. "You're stressing about nothing. I'll be home in an hour or two, I promise."

I heard her gulp on the other end of the line. "You're right," she whispered. "I'm probably just being silly. I have to go!" she added suddenly before slamming down the receiver. I cringed, the sound doing nothing for my headache. *Thanks, Pippa.*

***

"Okay," I said out loud to myself as I swept the last of the mess into the trash hours later. "It might be fun to be busy occasionally, but I really need to find some more staff. Today was just ridiculous."

I let myself out the back and locked the door, barely even aware of what I was doing as I stumbled towards my car.

Suddenly a body stepped in front of me.

I screamed. Boy, I really was jumpy these days.

"Sorry, it's only me," a gruff male voice called out. I could see him holding his hands up in the dark. "I came back to collect my final check."

I thought Romeo had some nerve coming back to collect money, but at the same time, I didn't begrudge him the money that he had actually earned.

I nodded and sighed. "Come on in, I just need to

unlock the door again."

He followed me back into the bakery and to my office where his check lay on my desk.

I paused just as I was about to hand the check over. "So are you going to tell me why you stormed out that day? You kind of left us in the lurch here. I'm asking because I am genuinely worried that we did something to upset you, Romeo."

He grabbed the check out of my hand and stared at the tiles. "I just wasn't happy here," he said, before glancing up at me with guilty-looking eyes. "Sorry that I left like that, though. I do appreciate you taking the chance with hiring me."

I sighed. "Something must have really upset you that day. Was it just because I was late getting back with your coffee? I know the early hours can be a drag..."

Romeo let out a little laugh and shook his head. "It wasn't that, Rachael." He started to walk back out.

"Just tell me then," I called out. "Look, we're really overlaoded here lately. If you want your job back, I'm willing to give you another chance."

He spun back around. "After what I did?"

I sighed. "I know. I'm not a total pushover, just let

me make that clear. But I do believe in second chances. Plus, we're kind of desperate," I had to admit.

He stared at me for a long while before finally shaking his head. "Sorry, Rachael. It's nothing personal, but I can't work here."

"Why not?" I asked, chasing him as he left out the back via the kitchen. We were out in the dark alley before he finally answered.

"Why don't you ask, Pippa."

Then he spun around and disappeared into the dark night.

Ask Pippa? What did Pippa do to make him leave?

I threw my head back in a silent scream. I had a pretty good idea. She could frighten anyone away.

Maybe it wasn't Gus who was making up the ghost stories to drive people away. Maybe the real culprit had been living in my home the entire time.

***

"Pippa!" I called out as I stormed into the apartment. I threw my coat onto the hall table and stepped over the broken glass shards that were still lying in the hall, even though I could have sworn we'd cleaned all of them up. "I need to talk to you!"

But Pippa wasn't in her usual spot on the sofa. "Pippa?"

I found her shivering on top of my bed with only a lamp on besides her. "What's happened, Pippa? Have you caught my flu?" She was holding the blanket up to her face, and she was white and pale and clammy when I felt her forehead.

"Rachael...I...I..." Her teeth were chattering too hard for her to be able to speak properly.

Shoot. Something was really wrong with her. "Do you need to go to the hospital?" I wrapped the blanket around her tighter, hoping that would stop the shivering.

She shook her head. "I'm not sick, Rachael."

I sat down besides her, understanding now. "Pippa, what's frightened you so much?" I felt a stab of guilt over the fact I hadn't come home as soon as she'd called me. "Sorry, Pips. I should have left the mess to clean up in the morning."

Pippa was still shivering as she stared off into the

distance. "I saw something, Rachael," she whispered.

I stood up, thinking about the glass shards in the hallway. "Did someone break in?" I asked, terrified as well now.

"Not someone," Pippa whispered. "Rachael, the thing I saw wasn't alive, it wasn't human."

I stomped over and turned the lights on properly. "Come on, Pippa," I said. "You're freaking me out."

"I don't mean to," she whispered. Her eyes were filled with tears now. One of them spilled down her cheek. "I'm not making it up, though. Rachael, there was a ghost in the house. I heard something in the hall. I went to investigate, and I saw it."

I was fighting not to show that I was scared as well, but I was losing the battle. "Pippa, I think you've just caught my flu," I said gently, completely forgetting about all the drama with Romeo earlier. "Maybe you're just hallucinating?" I asked hopefully.

She shook her head. "I feel fine. Besides, have you been hallucinating?"

No, I had just been feeling sick to my stomach. No ghostly apparitions.

"Rachael." Pippa tried to steady her voice. "It told me

to stay away from Gus's shop."

I just stood there staring at her.

I wasn't sure what I believed at that moment.

"Pippa," I said gently, but firmly. "I know you're scared right now, but you have to admit that sounds a little ridiculous. After all the crazy stuff you've had in your head, don't you think it's possible that maybe you just imagined it?"

She shook her head. "That's it, Rachael, I'm out."

"Out of what?"

"The investigation for one thing. No more snooping around at night, no more asking questions. I'm done with all of it. And if you want my advice, you should leave it alone as well." She shot me a look. "And if you decide to go ahead with buying Gus's shop, then I am done with the bakery as well."

Chapter 7

So now there was one. Just me, alone, trying to solve this mystery. Gus was still my prime suspect.

I had found out earlier from another shop owner on our street that the guy who was murdered was someone named Jason Hamilton. I knew a lot of people in this town, with my business and living here as long as I have, and I was thankful that I didn't know him. The shop owner from the yarn store, Knitwit, had told me that the police weren't releasing his name, but she had found out from her brother-in-law that works at the station. That explained why Jackson wouldn't answer any of my questions about the murder victim. It was supposed to be all hush-hush.

I sat down at my kitchen table and got out a notebook. It was still hours before Pippa would rise so I knew I had a little time before she caught me. I started scribbling down the ideas I had so far.

Access. Gus owns the shop, so he had the opportunity to kill Jason.

Motive. Gus has a big motive for killing Jason. He wants to keep his shop. The murder—and the freaky stories surrounding it—means that no one will want to buy the shop.

I paused and put the pen to my lips. Hmm. *In fact, the stories could actually attract more attention to his store. People like antiques with a story. And it would also buy him a little time before he has to sell.*

I glanced at Pippa sleeping over my shoulder. All of a sudden, I was desperate to wake her up and tell her my theory. She'd thought that Gus wouldn't make up ghost stories because it would be bad for business.

But what if they were actually *good* for his line of business?

But Pippa had said she was done with the case. Sadly, I turned around and let her sleep. I was going to have to do this on my own.

"What are you doing?"

"Nothing!" I slammed the notebook shut. "Just writing down a list of stock we have to order for the wedding reception."

Pippa frowned. "The reception? The one that's today? A little late to be ordering supplies, isn't it?"

"Just a few last minute things I need to get. The bride had some special gluten free requirements for some of the guests."

"Oh," Pippa said, nodding. "We don't want to poison any of the guests." She cringed. "Sorry. Poor choice of words." The memory of a customer being poisoned— and one of my pies being to blame—was still a little too fresh. But I told her not to worry about it.

"We need to get going. It's big days like this that can really make or break the bakery!"

***

"Hey, you guys are opening really late today," a man wearing an army jacket and a bright yellow hat said as he waited by the bakery door. I pulled out my key, struggling as I juggled boxes of the gluten free supplies I'd been forced to buy while Pippa accompanied me to the specialty store. That's what I got for lying: three hundred dollars out of pocket. Oh well, the reception we were about to host would make up for that little loss.

"Sorry," I said, putting on an apologetic face as I struggled with my boxes. "We're closed for a private function this afternoon. Hence the late start. A wedding reception."

"Oh," the man said, scowling as he craned his neck to try and get a look through the window. "That sounds mighty interesting. Is anyone welcome to come along?"

Out of respect for my guests' privacy, I stood in front of him. "No, sorry." But I couldn't help thinking what a strange request that was. Who asked that? "We'll be open to the public again tomorrow morning. I hope to see you then!"

I wasn't sure I really was, but I watched him trudge away.

"Who was that?" Pippa asked.

"An unwanted guest," I said. "Wow!" My breath was almost taken away by how beautiful the inside of the bakery looked, all decked out in pink, silver, and white. "You did an amazing job, Pippa."

She grinned at me. "Let's get ready this wedding reception!"

I was dressed to match the decor in a short pink and silver dress, partly because I wanted to blend in with the scenery. I was there as staff, not as a guest. Still, it was exciting to see the bakery come to life like that, to see it full of people dancing and eating and enjoying themselves. I cast a glance next door. If only we'd been able to use the second store, we could have fit in even more guests.

"What are you thinking about?" Pippa nudged me and nibbled on a cupcake.

"Nothing," I said quickly, straightening up. "Just admiring the shop."

"Why don't you take a break?" She winked at me, though I had no idea why. "Something tells me that you might want to have a dance soon."

"Does it?" I asked incredulously. "Pippa, I'm here to serve food, not dance it up!"

She nudged me again and then pointed at the crowd before scooting away. I turned to see what on earth she was pointing at.

My eyes widened and I straightened up immediately. How long had he been standing there?

"Jackson!" I'd seen him in a suit before, his detective suit, but this was different. Usually he wore dark colors but today he was dressed in a rather festive light grey with a salmon colored tie. It suited him.

"I had no idea you were going to be here."

"The groom and I are friends from way back," Jackson explained. "But I don't know too many of the guests, I have to admit, but when I saw the reception was being held here, I just had to tag along."

He did know how to make a girl blush.

"Would you join me for a quick dance?"

I glanced around. Would it be incredibly bad form for a server to join in? But the bride nodded at me and I took that as a sign that I had her permission. However, I was still a little nervous about dancing with Jackson for some reason.

"Hey, you never told me why you ran out of the coffee shop the other day," Jackson said as we gently swayed to a mid-tempo pop song.

I shot him a look. "I just didn't like being accused, that's all."

"I told you, I wasn't accusing you of anything." He was silent for a moment. "Though there were some rumors that you were sneaking around the crime scene shortly afterwards."

I pulled back. "So you *are* accusing me then?"

"Not of having anything to do with that man's murder."

"What are you accusing me of then?"

He raised an eyebrow. "Trying to solve the case

yourself."

I felt my face go red and we began to dance again.

"Am I wrong?"

I shook my head. "No," I admitted softly. "But I have a personal stake in this, Jackson. I was already supposed to be the owner of that shop by now. Then all this happened."

Jackson frowned. "You do realize you're not a detective though, Rachael. Do you have your PI's license?"

"No," I had to admit. "But anyone can be an amateur sleuth, can't they?"

He sighed. "I just don't want you to get into trouble again.

I wondered if it was already too late for that. There was no way I wanted to get into all the paranormal stuff—sorry, alleged paranormal stuff—with Jackson, but so much creepy stuff had happened lately that I was starting to wonder if I really should back off and listen to Pippa.

"You've gone awful quiet."

"Just enjoying a bit of peace," I said quietly.

The DJ started playing a more upbeat song and I took that as my cue to pull away again. "Sorry, I just need to run out for a second. See if we have any cakes left in the back." Really, I needed to go to the bathroom, but he didn't need to know that.

"Okay," Jackson said, looking disappointed.

As soon as I finished in the bathroom and headed back to the counter, Pippa shot me a look. "What are you doing? Go back over to him!"

I turned around. Jackson was dancing a little awkwardly by himself in the middle of the floor. "I don't know." Just as I was contemplating going back over to him, there was a loud crashing sound.

That's when we all heard the screams coming from next door.

***

"Move away," Jackson commanded as all the guests spilled from my shop to Gus's, all trying to rubberneck and see what was going on.

I tried to push through the crowd. "What is it?" I asked Jackson.

"You too," he commanded. "Rachael, you need to step back." It seemed like the intimacy between us had faded away already.

I looked past him anyway. I had to see what the heck was going on.

I brought my hands to my mouth and gasped as I saw it: a dead body lying in the center of Gus's Antiques. From the looks of it, a young woman.

Another murder victim.

***

"Well, that kind of put a dampener on the whole wedding reception." Pippa sat next to me while I tried to soothe my nerves with a cup of ginger tea. It wasn't working. The guests had all cleared out and I hadn't even collected payment from the bride and groom.

"What a total disaster," I groaned, throwing my head on the table.

"Not to mention a tragedy," Pippa pointed out.

"I know, I know." I looked up. "You can go if you like. Jackson said he only needed me to stick around."

Pippa wasn't above making a joke in that moment. "I bet he did."

"He just wants to ask me a few questions."

On top of everything else, I was incredibly nervous about why he wanted to speak to me. But I told Pippa I was fine and that she ought to go home.

It seemed like I was waiting hours for Jackson to finally come speak to me. "Thanks for waiting. Sorry your event got ruined."

"You ought to tell that to the bride and groom."

He sat down across from me and pulled a notepad out of his breast pocket. "Did you see anything suspicious today before you started work?"

I thought for a second before shaking my head. "I was in a rush. Nothing that I can remember." I paused. "Jackson, how did she die?"

"I told you earlier, we can't give out that information to the public."

I'd been hoping I was more than just 'the public.' "But how can I help you if I don't know any of the details of how she died?"

"And I've told you that already as well: you don't need to help us in that way. You can help by answering my questions."

I leaned forward. "Did she die the same way as the first victim? Do you think we are looking for the same person?"

What I really wanted to ask was, *Do you already have an idea of the suspect? Because the first person you should be looking for is Gus.*

He glared at me. "Rachael, 'we' are not looking for anyone. The police are looking for a suspect. You'd do better to stay out of it. Now, can you remember anything suspicious happening today?"

I shook my head and stood up. "I really should be getting home, if that's all."

He looked at me gravely. "It's not, actually."

I turned back to him in surprise. "I've already told you I didn't see anything. What else do you want from me?"

"I'm sorry to do this, Rachael. But if you don't want to cooperate here, I'm afraid I'm going to have to ask you to come down to the station to ask a few more questions. Officially."

I just stared at him. "You've got to be kidding me, Jackson. I was here the whole time!"

He stared at me. "Not the whole time."

I rolled my eyes. The bathroom break. Right before the screams. I shook my head. This was just great.

"Fine. You lead the way."

Chapter 8

I felt like I had been in the back of the police car for an eternity. Jackson mentioned something about the storm coming and I stared at the dark clouds above that looked like they were about to engulf the entire town of Belldale with one swallow.

But all I felt was numb. I pressed my cheek against the glass to try to feel something. "Can I roll down a window?" The heat in the car was suffocating.

"It's about to start raining," Jackson replied, sounding slightly curt.

I took it as a no.

Guilty. That's the way I felt. A second body? I glanced down and played with the bracelet on my wrist, spinning it round and round. What if I really was to blame?

What if Pippa was right?

Either way, it seemed like everything I'd worked so hard for was slipping away again. Just when things seemed to be going well, disaster struck again.

What if I really was cursed?

***

The seat was plastic and digging into my back. Now I was freezing. Would it have killed them to put on the heat? It was the middle of winter, after all, and we were about to be hit by a storm.

But I supposed cops didn't really care about making their suspects feel comfortable.

"Gus Sampson is the person you should be questioning."

It was a different detective interviewing me this time, a woman in her early thirties with a rail thin frame and curly red hair. "Where is Detective Jackson, by the way?"

She paused from the notes she was jotting down and shot me a look. "He's busy. You don't need to worry about him."

I wondered if he'd asked this woman—Detective Emma Crawford, apparently—to conduct the interview because he had a conflict of interest concerning me.

"So," Detective Crawford said. I wondered how long she had worked at the station. If her and Jackson were partners. If they ever worked cases together, long nights on stakeouts...

"You were in the bathroom?" She raised a thinly manicured eyebrow. "That's a convenient story."

"Not very convenient seeing as I am in here," I pointed out.

"Can anybody confirm you were using the bathroom?"

I shook my head. I didn't want to say anything else. I wanted to speak to Jackson. Or get a lawyer.

Detective Crawford continued.

"And weren't you also a suspect in the murder of Colleen Batters?"

"Emphasis on suspect. For about a minute. I actually helped to solve that case," I said pointedly.

A look of amusement crossed her face. "Did you? That's nice that you think that."

I felt like I had shrunk to the size of a mushroom. Maybe I wasn't a cop, and maybe I didn't officially have a P.I's license, but I had helped to solve that murder fair and square.

I crossed my arms. "You can ignore what I have to

say about Gus Sampson, but if you do, it's at your own peril." I knew how ridiculous that sounded before I'd even got to the end of the sentence and immediately wished I could reach out for the words and swallow them.

Detective Crawford's amusement only grew wider. "I think we'll be okay."

I nodded, silent again. After everything that happened, I wasn't sure I was doing much good towards the case anyway. I hadn't been able to stop the second girl from dying.

"Did you even come into contact with Bridget Lassiter before?"

"Bridget?" I asked, confused.

Detective Crawford blinked slowly. "That's the name of the woman who was found dead today."

I ran the name through my head, foraging for a connection, but I just ended up shaking my head. "Was she the same age as the other victim?"

Another long blink. "Roughly the same. Don't try to solve this case for us. Detective Whitaker said you had a habit of that."

I raised an eyebrow. So he talked about me to her.

Maybe to others.

I leaned forward. "With all due respect,Detective, there are two people dead. Will there be more to come? If you want my opinion, the sole person you should be looking at is Gus Sampson." I told the detective about what I had seen him doing in his store that morning, with the painting and the wires.

She frowned. "You saw him jiggling a painting around? Sounds very suspicious." I could tell she was biting her lip to keep from laughing now. I realized that without context, without explaining to her everything about the painting and the so-called 'curse'—and, most importantly, without explaining that I had broken into his shop the night before—that Gus playing with the wires on the painting added up to exactly zero evidence against him.

I leaned back. Maybe what I'd seen did mean exactly nothing.

But Gus had to have done it. "It's not just the painting thing," I pointed out, worried that I sounded totally stupid now. "He's the only person with access to the store." I saw the look on her face. "Well, apart from the other employees of course," I added quietly. Maybe I really was out of my depth here.

"Don't you think we, as detectives, have already thought of that?"

"Most likely," I mumbled. "Yes."

Detective Crawford stood up and opened the door for me. She had a small smile on her face that seemed genuine. "You're free to go, Rachael."

"I am?" I asked, surprised, as I stood up after her. I buttoned up my coat. "I take it this means I am no longer a person of interest."

She cast me a long steely gaze. "Just make sure you come to us if you see anything else interesting or suspicious. You do run the bakery next door to the crime scene, after all."

I stopped buttoning. "Does this mean that you'd like me to be your eyes and ears out there?"

"We don't need your help with solving the case, if that's what you're getting at, Miss Robinson. And don't try to solve it yourself. Just tell us if you see anything."

I did try to tell you what I saw. But you weren't interested, I thought as she showed me the door. *You practically laughed at what I'd seen.*

But I knew that what I'd seen—Gus tampering with that painting—meant something. I just didn't know what that was yet.

But I couldn't quell that nagging feeling in my stomach that it *was* important and that Gus needed to be brought in off the streets before anyone else ended up dead.

But if Detective Crawford wasn't going to listen to me, what more could I do?

I should have been relieved at being set free and taken off the suspect list, but I only felt stupid as I stumbled out of the interview room, like I was a little kid playing at being a detective and a grownup had told me off and told me to stop pretending.

That's why I almost stumbled into the figure heading towards me. He was super familiar, but it took me a moment to place the dark-haired man staggering into the interview room after me.

"Romeo?" I whispered out loud. "What the heck is he doing here?"

I spun around only to see him being led into the room.

Maybe he saw something.

But if he was at the bakery, why? Was he snooping around again? I thought about the night I'd bumped into him out back when I was closing up. He'd claimed he was there to get his paycheck, but he could have been doing anything and just used that as a cover when he was caught.

I shivered at the idea that I'd ever let him work in my bakery as I stared at the closed door of the interview room.

"Can I help you, miss?" a weary-looking uniformed police officer asked, grabbing my attention. "You look a little lost there."

I straightened up. "I'm just looking for Detective Whitaker. To say goodbye to him before I leave." Sort of true. I was thinking that, if one detective wouldn't listen to me, maybe another one would. I'd already *slightly* tested the waters with Jackson regarding the curse, and I figured that if I explained the entire thing to him, he might be a little more open-minded to listen to the curse as a theory.

Boy, I was starting to sound like Pippa.

"Can't help you, sorry. I think he's busy at the moment." The uniformed officer returned to the magazine he was reading.

Really busy or just 'doesn't want to see me' busy? I wondered.

"Thank you."

"Exit's that way."

Right.

I bumped into him as I was exiting the station.

"Jackson!" He looked a little pleased to see me, I was sure of it, but he looked around uneasily to check if anyone was watching us. "I have to tell you something. Detective Crawford wouldn't listen to me about something I saw."

He looked at me blankly. "She should have listened to you, if you had some kind of witness evidence to put forth."

I didn't want to get her into trouble. "No! It's not like that. I suppose I don't really blame her for not listening. Do you have five minutes?"

I wished Pippa was with me as I unraveled the entire story to him, ending with the way I'd seen Gus jiggling around the 'haunted' painting the following morning. "I'm not going to be arrested for trespassing, am I?"

"Trespassing?" he asked. "No. What you did was breaking and entering."

My face turned white. "I was only trying to help. The

door was open when Pippa and I went in, anyway, so it wasn't breaking in." A quick lie to try and save us from getting booked.

Jackson shook his head. "That's besides the point right now. Obviously, we had Gus Sampson as a suspect."

My ears pricked. "Did you say 'had'? Why the past tense?"

Jackson glanced into the station. Boy, he really did not want anyone to see us together, did he?

Jackson sighed. "I shouldn't really be telling you this, but given everything." He placed his hands in his pockets. "Gus is out of town right now, meeting up with an antique dealer in Pottsville. We have confirmation of his alibi already. He's been out of town all weekend." Jackson stared down at my face draining of more and more color by the second. "Gus wasn't there, Rachael. He couldn't have done it."

My head started spinning.

"Okay," I said unsteadily. "I need to go then. Sorry." I hurried away, pushing my way through the glass doors, but I didn't think the apology was really necessary. I doubted he was very sorry to see me go at that point.

I gulped for air when I finally got outside.

If Gus Sampson hadn't killed those two people, then who? Or what?

Detective Crawford might have said I was free to go, and I doubted I'd be called in for questioning again, but I couldn't help the feeling of guilt that twisted in my stomach.

Was I responsible for those people getting killed?

What if...what if the curse was real? What if my decision to purchase the antiques shop had set in motion a chain of events that had lead to the deaths of two innocent people?

I glanced back at the police station right as thunder cracked overhead. I wanted to run back in there, turn myself in, present my wrists, and say 'Lock me up, I'm a hazard to the community.'

But that would be insane. I backed away.

Perhaps there was somewhere else I really needed to go. A place I had been avoiding.

And dreading.

But I needed answers.

Chapter 9

I wasn't sure I'd ever even BEEN in this area of Belldale before. The town had a population of only about fourteen thousand, but it was divided by a small highway that split the two into two distinct halves and this half was one I was unfamiliar with. There were coffee shops I didn't recognize, and the streets seemed wider with the shops more spread out. It was at least a ten-minute drive from our apartment, but Pippa seemed to know exactly where she was going.

She'd been there many times before.

'Downtown', I suppose the area would be called.

We finally pulled up behind an innocuous-looking building.

"This is it?" I wasn't sure if I was disappointed or relieved.

The meeting place didn't look anywhere near as spooky as I was expecting it to. I had imagined the club met in a cave surrounded by cobwebs or something.

But this was just a spare room in the back of a regular-looking church on a Monday night. There were a few cobwebs, sure, and there was a musty smell like the place hadn't been aired out in months or years, but there was nothing gothic or scary about it.

"I know. I was a little disappointed at first as well. But it does the job we need it to."

I took in a deep breath. I wondered if it would do the job I needed it to. Or whether I was finally losing my mind, going down the rabbit hole that Pippa had already been dragged into by Tegan and her ilk.

"We have to pay fifty dollars to use the space every week," Pippa explained as she began to unfold chairs. "We take donations of people when they come through the door." She set me up at a little folding table with instruction to take people's money and put it in an old pickle jar. Around here, Pippa was my boss.

"Why don't you just meet at the house of one of the members?" I asked.

"You'll see," Pippa said, raising her eyebrow.

I did see. I was expecting a handful of people at the meeting, five or six at the most. But as soon as the clock hit 4:30, people began streaming into the small room and within twenty minutes, the entire place was full wall to wall of members of the clearly very popular Belldale Paranormal Society.

I gulped.

I get claustrophobic around large groups of people and suddenly wasn't sure this was such a good idea.

"Rachael," an eerie voice called out. Tegan had finally sauntered into the room right at five. She still had her cape on, but some of the purple had faded from her hair, revealing blonde roots.

Pippa raised an eyebrow at me. "You two have met before?"

"I'm so glad you finally decided to join us at one of our meetings. I think you will find it very enlightening. I've been hoping to see you here for quite some time." Tegan closed and locked the door behind her and everyone went quiet as she swished her way to a small podium in the middle of the back wall. "

Pippa quietly took the jar from me and quickly counted it. When she was done, sh nodded to Tegan.

I shivered. Now that the sun had gone down, a kind of spooky quality had taken over the room. It was freezing and Pippa had to set up a tiny space heater in the corner, which barely did anything but did add an interesting smell to the room, sort of like burning plastic but slightly more sinister.

Or maybe it was just Tegan's presence that had changed the make-up of the room. She had a knack for doing that.

There were all sorts of people in the club. Some were relatively normal-looking, still wearing suits and ties from work, but the majority of them wore items that would immediately get them labeled as 'alternative' to onlookers. Necklaces with pentagons and other symbols that I didn't quite recognize, hair dyed in various bright, unearthly shades.

I suddenly saw how well Pippa fit in here. And she seemed very 'at home,' milling amongst everyone, talking and chatting and catching up with gossip that I wasn't privy to. I couldn't help but feel a little jealous that Pippa had friends she was just as close with, or even closer to, than me.

I settled into an empty seat beside her. The others were being friendly enough, saying hello, introducing themselves, but I still felt distinctly ill at ease. I was so far out of my element it wasn't funny.

"You don't need to look so nervous, Rach. These people don't bite. They are just interested in discussing and learning about all the unexplained paranormal happenings in Belldale." She gave me a grin. "Just a bunch of amateur detectives, kind of like you!"

She patted my hand and I nodded. Maybe that was true. Everyone in the club was here because they had a thirst to solve the unsolvable, an interest in puzzles and the unknowable. But I still felt uneasy as I waited for Tegan to begin.

Before she'd started talking, I had no idea there were so many unexplained mysteries in Belldale. We were just one little town, but apparently we had a very storied history. This week, there was a lot of discussion focused on this so called 'mystical big cat' that many members of the town—and specifically the club— claimed to have seen, but no one had ever actually caught or taken a proper photo of. Belldale's very own Bigfoot. Apparently, this creature was black with bright red eyes and was capable of disappearing right in front of a person's eyes. There had been fresh sightings this week.

"I saw it dissolve into thin air," a young man named Aaron, with long dark hair and a sleeve of tattoos, piped up. "While I was trying to take a photo of it." A little too convenient for my tastes.

But others had similar stories.

"All of this can't possibly be true, can it?" I

whispered to Pippa. She returned an eager nod.

"Of course. You see why I like it here now?"

I had to admit there was a certain appeal to it all. The human mind is drawn to mysteries and, by extension, the paranormal. All the stories were fascinating, but I had to remind myself to keep a skeptical mind. But as I listened to the club discuss everything from large cats to haunted houses and even alleged UFO sightings, I felt my nerves dissolve a little. In fact, I totally forgot myself for a while and just sat there and listened.

"See, Rach?" Pippa whispered to me. "You'll never have to worry about being bored and not having a mystery to solve ever again—if you just keep coming to these meetings!"

She was probably right. Maybe I would have to keep coming along.

But I wasn't sure this was entirely where I belonged. I felt like a tourist in that room, listening to everyone's strange stories but feeling two steps removed from them all.

Tegan eventually drifted the topic onto the next part of the meeting, and I was still so distracted thinking about all the mysterious 'cases' that had been brought up that I jumped when I heard my name mentioned.

"Now, Rachael is going to tell us all a very interesting story!" Tegan placed her hands together and nodded at me while everyone clapped.

I am? I thought. "Pippa, you never told me I had to stand up in front of people and talk to them."

"Then stay seated while you talk," she answered, rather unhelpfully. "Come on. This is what you came for, right? For help? How are you going to get any if you won't tell your story?"

I sighed a little and stood up. I took a deep breath. Public speaking isn't that bad...is it?

Yes, it is. It's basically the worst thing imaginable.

I headed up to the podium. Tegan's eyes were still boring into me. I tried to relax and ignore her—and everyone else in the room—and just focus on Pippa in the audience. She was grinning at me and nodding her support.

Here goes nothing.

Everyone looked enraptured as I unleashed my story. I told them all about the day I'd decided to buy Gus's antiques store, and how the—I paused before I said the word '*curse*'—seemed to have started right after then.

"And, Rachael, have you been feeling sick all the time?" Tegan's voice called out.

I paused for a second. "Yes," I had to admit. "Almost constantly, actually."

Tegan nodded and I could hear her murmuring, "A clear sign of a curse."

Was it? I took a moment before I got to the really juicy detail of the story; the salacious events that I knew everyone was really there to hear about.

I gulped right before I spoke. "Then, of course, there are the murders."

There were a few gasps and murmurs in the crowd.

Tegan's eyes drilled into me as I told them about the two bodies that had been found in Gus's antique store. First the man Jason, then the second, a woman named Bridgett. "They were both found in the antique shop next to her bakery. It looks as though the killer was the same person."

I could have sworn that Tegan was shooting me a judgmental look. The severity of it took me off guard and I stammered for a moment as I tried to remember what I was talking about. I felt as though I should clear something up for the crowd. "Even though I was taken in for questioning, I was quickly released. Er, thank you." There was some thin applause as I scampered back to my seat.

Tegan looked grim as she retook to the podium. "As you can see, something rather terrible has befallen Rachael. A curse!"

Everyone nodded and half the crowd turned to look at me. I could feel my face growing red. "And we can help her," Tegan added. "Don't worry, Rachael." She turned her full attention to me now. "You're in the right place now, a safe place. We can remove this curse that has taken over your life. If you will accept our help."

She seemed to be waiting for an answer or confirmation from me. The room was silent as everyone stared at me.

I sat very still. Eventually I nodded, and a sly smile spread over Tegan's face. I was willing to try anything.

At this stage, I was willing to believe just about anything. After all, anything could be possible. And I was running out of rational explanations for all the weird stuff that had been happening to me.

Pippa reached over and squeezed my hand. "You'll be fine now. Everything will go back to normal if you just follow their instructions."

But little did I know, I was NOT about to like the advice that Tegan was going to give me.

"First of all," she announced. "You are going to have to go back and undo any of the actions you made that caused the curse to be placed on you."

"Well, I don't have a time machine," I half-joked, though no one seemed to find this amusing. So I sat still and silent again.

"Do you still have that contract you signed?" Tegan looked at me pointedly.

Did she mean the sales contract? I nodded uneasily.

"Good. Burn it."

Burn it? That seemed a little extreme and melodramatic.

I turned towards Pippa, who was nodding enthusiastically. I bet she was loving this advice. Her eyes did seem to be lighting up.

Tegan continued, "Next you have to go into the shop and apologize to the twins' spirits."

"You mean the painting?" I asked, slightly incredulous.

"I mean the spirits that placed the curse on you." She meant the painting, though. I sat back in my seat.

"Take back all the intentions you made to buy the property and try to offer them something in order to remove the bad karma. A gift or a sacrifice."

But I was still caught up on the first point. "Take back all my intentions? Burn the contract? You're telling me..." I shot a look at Pippa. "That I can't buy the store?" I started to get this little nagging feeling in the pit of my stomach that Pippa had put Tegan up to this. It all seemed to align exactly with what she had been nagging me to do.

Tegan looked outraged. "Why on Earth would you still wish to purchase the store after there have been two murders in there? You need to cancel all your plans immediately."

She had a fair point. I'd been considering that myself. Who wants to eat in a bakery where there have been two murders?

I'd been trying to tell myself that if I could just prove that the killer was human, that there is no curse, no ghosts, it isn't so bad.

I hung my head and whispered to Pippa. "Maybe she has a point. Maybe you have a point. Maybe I really have

102

to rethink my business plan."

I glanced up to see Pippa exchanging a wink with Tegan, and mouthing the word "thanks."

I stood up. "So you did put Tegan up to this then? You told her to say that to me?"

Pippa looked aghast. "Rach, what are you getting so upset for? You know this is the right thing to do. What, where are you going?"

"I'm leaving, Pippa. I came here for real advice, not to be set up. You know what? It sounds to me as though you've been against my plan from the start! What is it, Pippa? What is really going on? Why did you tell Tegan to say all of that stuff?"

"Rachael, I can explain." She looked startled as I started to stomp out of the room. She shrugged apologetically at Tegan and started to chase after me. "Please, just stay for the rest of the meeting. These guys are really cool once you get to know them, I promise."

I pulled on my coat. "No. You can either come with me now or stay with these guys and catch the bus home later."

"You need me to drive," she pointed out. My old car didn't have GPS and I'd had to rely on her to get to the meeting.

"I can find my way."

Pippa sighed. "I'll just come with you. Hang on."

I was still fuming once we got to the car. "So are you going to tell me what is really going on?"

"I've already told you a thousand times before," Pippa said, "There's an evil spirit behind all of this! Or spirits. How else do you explain everything? I thought you were willing to keep an open mind." Pippa's face crumbled in distress. "I was so excited when you told me you wanted to come to the meeting. I thought you were finally willing to accept that all this stuff is true."

***

We didn't talk much during the car ride home. Of all the people I could possibly lose trust in, Pippa was the worst. We'd always been there for each other. But now I was starting to think there was some other reason she didn't want me to buy Gus's shop and she was just using this so-called 'curse'—and Tegan—to scare me off.

I finally broke the silence once we were back in my kitchen. "I'm not sure which is worse, Pippa: you lying to me about this curse, or you actually believing all this crazy stuff."

Pippa stared back at me for a long while. "Okay, yes, I did tell Tegan to advise you not to buy the shop! But I was trying to protect you, Rachael!"

I shook my head. "I knew it."

"I do believe in all this stuff that you call crazy," she finally whispered, a little sadly. "I just wish you could see it. I wish you would listen to Tegan."

"Pippa, can't you see? This club is getting in your head. And worse than that, it's getting in the way of our friendship." I shook my head. "We've been bickering for weeks now, and it's always about the same thing. I wish you would just use your brain for a second and see how illogical all of this crazy stuff is."

I stomped over to the fridge and grabbed some leftover cake from the shelf. That plan to eat more fruits and vegetables had been a failure so far. "From now on, I'm going back to solving this mystery the old fashioned way. Looking for suspects... human suspects! And finding evidence. See, Pippa, there's one crucial aspect that has been missing from all these paranormal theories, and that is evidence! These so-called friends of yours are not your friends, Pippa, if they make you lose touch with reality."

Pippa was just staring at me with her hands on her hips. It seemed like she was trying to get up the guts to say something to me.

"Maybe if you actually had a little time for me lately, Rachael, I wouldn't have needed to make these new friends."

"What are you talking about?"

My stomach had begun to ache again and I stumbled over to the sink for a glass of water. I took a large gulp, but it did little to ease the pain.

"You've been so busy with the bakery the last year or so," Pippa started to chide. "Which I don't blame you for, of course. You had to take the time to build your business up. I get that. But I was hoping that when I started working there, it would be a chance for us to spend time together again. But you've barely even been at work! You've been so preoccupied with solving this case."

"Pippa, that's not true! We live and work together, for crying out loud! How much closer do you think we should be?"

"You didn't even know about my break up!" Pippa

blurted out. She immediately looked like she regretted it.

"What break up? I didn't even know that you were dating anyone."

How would she even have found time for that? And how could she have dated someone without me even knowing about it.

I suddenly realized.

"You were going out with Romeo?" My jaw was practically on the floor. Now his little fit made sense. It had nothing to do with the early mornings or the lack of caffeine in his system. It was a lover's tiff.

So that's what he'd meant that night when he'd told me to 'ask Pippa.'

Pippa was turning bright red as she looked at the floor. "I didn't think I could talk to you about it." But her voice was full of guilt, not accusations.

"You didn't think you could talk to me about it because you knew it was unprofessional of you to hire your boyfriend."

She nodded. "I thought that if you could just see what a good baker he was, you would be so pleased to keep him that you would overlook his questionable hiring."

I sighed. "That's why you were so nervous about me liking his baking." I shook my head. I wasn't angry with Pippa; I was just kind of hurt that she wouldn't be honest with me. Especially after I gave her the assistant manager job and bestowed the extra responsibilities onto her. I knew she'd always been kind of a flaky employee at the other places she'd worked, but I would have thought she'd know better than to hire her boyfriend at my bakery...and not even tell me about it.

"Rach?"

I sat down at the table and took another nibble of my cake. Pippa pulled out the chair besides me. "Aren't you going to say something?"

I stared at the table. "I was really worried about why Romeo had quit Pippa. I thought maybe I had done something to upset him." I shook my head. "I thought he'd been scared off by the tales about the ghost. Or the curse." I let out a little bitter laugh. "But it was all a lot more simple than that."

"Rachael, I'm sorry."

I swallowed. "Didn't you care that you were screwing with my business when you hired your boyfriend? Pippa, I'm down a baker now and we've been really struggling lately. Well, I'VE been struggling!"

Much to my horror, Pippa burst into tears. "I've been struggling as well, Rachael! I've just been trying not to show it!"

My phone began to ring.

"Rachael?" a familiar voice said. "There's been a break-in at your bakery. You ought to come down here."

Jackson ended the phone call without even saying goodbye.

***

There was broken glass all over the place, but nothing seemed to be missing. All the money in the register was still there and nothing had been taken.

Jackson took my statement anyway. "Is there anyone you think might have done this?"

Yeah, several, I thought. *Gus, Romeo, take your pick of the litter.*

"Hey, Jackson," a voice called out. "We found something."

I spun around to see Detective Crawford standing

109

there holding a broken video surveillance camera in her hands. "Looks like they were looking for this."

My security camera?

"Where does that footage go to?" Jackson asked in a super serious tone.

"It gets sent to my computer, an old laptop that I keep behind the counter. It's not good enough for anything else."

We both hurried behind the counter. Gone.

Someone had wanted that footage.

"Which way did this camera point?" Detective Crawford asked.

"Towards the street," I whispered quietly. I was starting to get an idea of why the thief had wanted it.

Detective Crawford glanced at Jackson. "We need to find that footage."

He nodded at her and they walked out together after Jackson advised me to take the following day off and to keep out of harm's way. The two of them looked rather cozy as they climbed back into their police car, I thought.

I sat down with unsteady legs at a table towards the

back. "I saw Romeo down at the police station when I was called in," I said quietly as Pippa joined me.

"What?" Pippa sat down next to me. "Why didn't you say anything?" Then she hung her head in her hands. "Oh no," she groaned.

"Oh no, what?"

Pippa sat upright. Her tears had dried up by this stage. "Oh, Rachael, I need to admit something to you."

I braced myself for a revelation about Tegan and the paranormal society.

But she had something quite different to reveal to me.

"Please don't be mad at me."

"Okay," I said unsurely. "Pippa, just tell me what it is."

"That night when I called you late at work...upset and crying..."

"I remember."

Pippa hung her head. "It was because of Romeo. He was at your apartment. We started to argue and he got angry again just like he did that day he stormed out of the bakery."

"Pippa, why didn't you tell me that!"

"I was embarrassed about all of it, Rach. It was easier to pretend I was scared of something paranormal than to admit to anything else."

I placed an arm around her. "It's okay, Pips. I'm just glad you aren't with the wretched guy anymore."

She dried her eyes and sat up. "Do you think it was him that broke in?"

I shook my head. "I have no idea. But promise me that you will stay away from him from now on?"

She nodded.

"How did you meet him anyway?" I asked.

Another look of guilt snuck over her face. "You aren't going to believe this, Rach."

"Oh, please don't tell me he is a member of the paranormal club?"

She shook her head. "No, but I did meet him while I was investigating something to do with the club." Her voice trailed off as she frowned.

"What were you investigating?"

She was quiet for a second. "The painting," she finally said. "In Gus's shop. Romeo was looking at it as well. He seemed super interested in it. I thought he might want to buy it so I had to warn him about it. So I told him all about the curse. He seemed really sweet and interested, so I kept talking and talking. He asked me out and we started dating."

I had to ask. "Pippa, is the reason you don't want me buying the shop because it has memories about Romeo?"

She let out a little laugh and shook her head. "No. Come on. I am a little more resilient than that."

She suddenly grew deadly serious. "But, Rachael, I have to tell you something. Even though I love this job and appreciate everything you've done for me. I'm sorry, but I have to tell you this. If you buy that shop, I *will* quit."

***

"Bronson...is it?" I asked, glancing over the guy's resume. He was young, but at least he already had a few years experience working in a bakery. Plus, he was here at 6:00 A.M. for an interview. You've got to want a job pretty badly if you're up and going at that hour. Plus, I was desperate.

The young man with the carrot-colored hair and freckles nodded eagerly. "That's right, miss." He had a rather charming southern accent. "I'm a quick learner. I can guarantee that you won't regret hiring me, ma'am."

I couldn't, not with the run of luck that I was having. "Can you start right away?"

I was just showing him into the kitchen when I heard the jingle that let me know we had a customer. "Sorry, we're not open for another hour or so...Jackson." I straightened up. "Sorry, Detective Whitaker. I assume you're here in an official capacity."

"Are you okay, Rachael? You're looking kind of green around the gills."

Great. Now the curse was turning me green on top of everything else. "Just a bit under the weather."

"Still? You really ought to see a doctor."

"Like I have time for that."

"Really. You have to go to one."

I nodded and promised to make an appointment as soon as he left. Not that it would do a lot of good. If I was cursed, what was a doctor going to do for me? I didn't say any of this to him, though.

Jackson cleared his throat. "Have there been any further incidents?"

"You mean has anybody else broken in? No."

He glanced around the room. "I thought I advised you not to open today."

"I chose to ignore that advice. Is there anything else I can do for you?"

Jackson leaned against the counter, his lips slightly pursed. "Have you seen Gus Sampson about?"

I shook my head. "I thought he was no longer a suspect."

Jackson looked down at the ground. "He's not." I could tell he wanted to say something, but was holding back.

I took a step closer and lowered my voice so that Bronson couldn't hear us. "Then who is?"

Jackson cleared his throat. "No one." He turned to leave. "Please let us know if you see Gus Sampson."

I narrowed my eyes. "Why? Is he still in Pottsville? Seeing that antiques dealer, right?"

"That's right," Jackson said. "As far as we know, anyhow."

He was just about to leave. "Hang on," I said suddenly. Jackson turned back to me. "If Gus is about to sell his shop—go out of business—then why is he out of town speaking to an antiques dealer?"

Jackson stood still for a moment. "That's actually a very good question."

I thought about it. "I suppose he could be, theoretically, buying for his own private collection. But with all the unsold stock he has, and his financial position, that seems unlikely."

"You're starting to think like a detective," Jackson replied. There was a hint of admiration in his voice, which surprised me.

"I thought you didn't like me sticking my nose in police business," I said playfully. "I thought you didn't want me having anything to do with this case."

"I never said that." He paused to correct him self. "Well, not recently. Your help did prove to be invaluable last time. I have to admit that. If you come up with something of interest again, I'd gladly listen to it."

I frowned. "Then why were you acting so cagey around me down at the station? Like you were afraid someone was going to see you talking to me? Seemed like you were kind of ashamed to be seen talking to me."

A blush of red crept up the sides of Jackson's neck. "That wasn't the reason for my furtiveness."

He didn't seem to want to continue. "Oh?" I prodded. "Pray tell then."

"I didn't want Detective Crawford to see me taking to you. I was afraid she might get the wrong impression."

"Right," I said. Now it was my turn to start blushing. So, they were seeing each other then.

"It's only recent, Rachael. We've only been on a couple of dates."

"Hey, it's none of my business."

I turned back towards the counter, performing my old trick of pretending I was cleaning a really stubborn stain out of the counter. The awkward silence hung between us both for a few moments.

"Hey," I said all casually, just as I sensed that Jackson was about to leave for good this time. "What was the name of the antiques dealer that Gus was meant to be visiting?"

"Maureen Tatler," he answered. "Why's that?"

"No reason. Just curious."

I could see from the look on his face that he regretted being so candid, regretting the accidental spilling of information that he otherwise would have guarded, if not for the desperate need to cut the awkward tension between the two of us.

I forced a smile at him as he backed out of the door. I thought he might tell me not to go to Pottsville. To leave well enough alone.

But he didn't.

And I wouldn't have listened to him even if he did.

***

"Gus!" I said, stopping with my car key in mid-air, pointed towards my car. "You're back."

"You sound disappointed," he said gruffly, stuffing his hands in his pockets. "Still keen to throw me out of my shop then?"

"No," I said, shaking my head. "It's not like that. It's never been like that Gus." I put my hand down and walked over to join him behind his shop. "I hope you don't think that. It's never been anything personal. I just want to expand my business." I nodded towards he store. "And this is the most convenient location."

He leaned against his own car. "Ah, I know that, sweetheart. It's just hard."

I wanted to bring up his trip to Pottsville without letting on how much I knew. "You've been away then?" I nodded towards the rear of his car, which was filled with luggage. "Was it a vacation?"

He let out a scoff. "Not exactly." He narrowed his eyes and shot me a sideways glance. "Actually, I was meeting up with someone who might be a little competition for you, if you really want to know."

"What do you mean? You were meeting with a baker?"

"No. Someone who might be interested in buying this joint." He nodded towards the shop. "And keep it in tact, not fill it with cakes and pastries."

Maureen Tatler. "Oh. So...what happened then?"

"Wouldn't you love to know?"

I would, actually.

Gus stood up straight. "You don't have to worry about her, sweetheart. Turns out she was only interested in buying one very specific item."

"Which item?" I asked quietly.

He shrugged. "Some painting of two little kids. But I told her, that painting ain't for sale."

***

My keys were already in the ignition and my car ready to pull out when a figure stepped in front of me, forcing me to slam on the brakes.

"You nearly gave me a heart attack!" I called out.

The guy, wearing army camouflage and a yellow hat, gave me a weary look before he continued walking like nothing had happened. I stared after him and watched him go through the back exit of Gus's Antiques.

I recognized him from somewhere, but it took me a moment or two to figure out where I had seen him before.

"Huh," I murmured. "That's strange. That's that guy that was there the morning of the wedding. The one who wanted to come in, that we turned away."

He never did come back the next day.

"Well," I said out loud, as I finally pulled out of the

parking lot. "I guess we're going on a road trip."

Chapter 10

Finally, I had something to go off of. I could have kissed Gus, I was so grateful for the tidbit that he had accidentally let slip about Maureen Tatler. There had to be a reason she wanted that painting. And it had to be connected to the killings.

There was no time to waste now. Word about the two homicides had spread around all of Belldale and it felt like history was repeating itself as our customer numbers dwindled down to a small trickle. People didn't feel safe venturing down to our once safe and cozy little enclave. And I didn't blame them. That was why I had to restore our reputation quickly. We needed to put the killer behind bars.

But I wasn't sure I could travel out to Pottsville on my own. Not without backup.

I needed Pippa's help.

More than that, I needed her company. I knew that once we actually got out on the road, and actually arrived in Pottsville, that Pippa would enjoy herself. It could be a chance for us to repair our friendship. I was even fairly sure that she'd enjoy investigating again once she was doing it. Especially if she knew the painting was involved.

I just needed to show her that.

So I had to rely on subterfuge.

I caught her just as she was pulling on her boots, about to head to another meeting of the Belldale Paranormal Society. "Hey, Pippa, you know how I haven't been feeling very well lately? I was thinking that some clean country air would do me a world of good. What do you say we get out of town for a day or two? Go on a little road trip, just the two of us?"

She sat up straight, a smile curling on her lips. "Are you serious?"

"Yeah. We should pack an overnight bag, throw it in the car and just drive out to the county, see what we find. How about out towards Pottsville?"

Pippa nodded thoughtfully. "But what about the bakery?"

"Bronson will be fine on his own for a couple of days." Normally I would never leave a new hire in charge of my business, but there was something about Bronson I felt like I could trust. Plus, we had very few customers these days.

"So what are we waiting for?"

Pippa's eyes widened. "What, you want to go right now? But I have a meeting! "

"This early?" I asked, looking at my watch. It was barely 7 A.M.

"We're meeting at Stanton Park to see if we can catch a glimpse of the mystical cat," Pippa said as she stuffed her camera and extra batteries in her purse. "Everyone knows he hunts in the morning."

I waved my hand dismissively. "Come on, you can miss one meeting. We may as well go now, make a long weekend of it."

It took us about three hours to reach Pottsville, an even smaller town than Belldale with a population of roughly four thousand people and a heavy reliance on apples as the prime source of industry and tourism. Neither of us had ventured there before, so it was new to both of us.

I had the name, Maureen Tatler. And I was pretty sure of the location, even though the old website Maureen had up only had the street name, not the full address of the house that also doubled as her place of business. And even though I had to rely on memorizing a map of the area before we left so that I could make my discovery of the street look totally innocent, I figured I would take my chances on both those fronts.

Halewood Road. I thanked my lucky stars that I'd been able to find it without driving around for hours or needing to make an excuse for why I needed to check my phone.

I pulled the car onto the street and slowed down until I saw what I was looking for.

That has to be it.

"Hey," I said, trying to sound both chirpy and casual. "This place looks cool. Looks like an old antiques dealer or something. Why don't we pull over and have a quick look inside?"

"I dunno, Rach, I've kind of had enough of antiques lately. Haven't you?"

Oh my gosh, yes. But I didn't say that. "This could be interesting though. And, come on, it's not like there's gonna be a wealth of things to do in this town."

She sighed. "Okay then, you've twisted my arm."

There was only one way to describe Maureen Tatler's house, and that was...haunted.

"It looks like a witch's castle," Pippa whispered as she stared up at the grey, gnarled building. She sounded more awe-struck than scared, though. "Tegan would LOVE this."

I suppressed my eye-roll. "You'll have to take some photos for her then. And for the rest of the club, since you missed the meeting. Get something to show them. So, are we going inside?"

I knocked on the door. "Hello?" Tapped again. There was no sound of movement on the other side of the door.

Pippa read out the plaque that hung beside the door. "Maureen Tatler, PhD. Antiques dealer and artist." Pippa paused. "It says her open hours are weekdays 9 - 4. So she should be inside."

I knocked again, harder this time, and the door pushed open thanks to the extra force.

Pippa and I looked at each other and shrugged. "Should we just go in?"

"What the heck is this place?" Pippa whispered as we moved through the dark creepy hallway. A spider's web hit my face and I cringed as I pulled off the sticky thread, shuddering at the thought that there might be a spider making its way down my shirt. Maureen clearly didn't have many buyers through the house. In fact, it seemed like no one had walked down this hall in weeks.

Months.

"Can you smell that?" Pippa asked. She'd always had a far more sensitive nose than me so it took a moment or two for me to realize what she was talking about.

"What IS that?" I had to cover my nose with my hand.

"It smells like something died in here."

***

"Maureen?" I called out.

Pippa had to run back to the car for a flashlight. We needed it as we entered the back of the property.

"I think we located the source of the smell," Pippa said, grimacing as she waved her hand in front of her face. "It's all this junk."

As she shone the flashlight over the room, I took in the stacks of newspapers and piles of old junk. I'd expected the property of an antiques dealer to be full of valuable items, collector's editions, stuff like armor and war memorabilia and hundred year old furniture. But this was just junk. Garbage that was festering and rotting, lining every inch of the room.

I still wasn't convinced that was what the smell was, though.

"How are we going to get through to the next room?"

We'd come to a dead end, a wall of newspapers blocking our way in the maze.

The papers smelled as bad as anything else in the house.

"I think we should just get the heck out of here," Pippa said. "This is dangerous, Rach. I don't know what we're here for anyway."

She turned to leave, but I grabbed her arm. "Wait, you can't go yet, Pippa. We have to find Maureen!"

She stared at me. "What's going on, Rachael?"

I was going to have to come clean or she was going to run out of there, leaving me to locate Maureen under a pile of garbage on my own. "I'm just worried about her, is all," I tried to say. "What if she's hurt? Or worse? We can't just leave her in this house in this state."

"Rachael, she's the one who made the mess. Looks like this is just how she lives. She's clearly a level five hoarder. This is not our monkey, and not our zoo. I don't want to die in here."

She made a move to leave and I grabbed her again. "Okay, fine. Just wait, Pippa. I need to tell you something."

I kept half an eye on the pile of newspaper, just waiting for it to tip over and crush us.

"Don't be mad, okay?" I tried to make Pippa promise me. "I only did this for our own good."

It looked like Pippa would not be able to make that promise. "Hurry up and tell me before we get killed in this joint, Rachael!"

I nodded. "Okay...okay...I drove us here on purpose. I wanted to find Maureen Tatler."

Pippa's mouth dropped open. "Why would you want to?" She sucked her breath in. "Right. Antiques dealer. Is this related to Gus? To the case?!" She shook her head and threw her head back. "Oh, I don't believe this, Rachael! I told you I was out! That I wanted nothing more to do with it!"

"But, Pippa," I tried to tell her as she started to stomp back towards the hallway. "It's about the painting. Maureen wants to buy it, but Gus won't sell. Don't you want to know why?"

"No, I don't!" she called out, her footsteps heavy as

she stomped away. "I can't believe you tricked me like this, Rachael!"

"Pippa, I'm sorry!"

I started to chase after her when I saw a ghostly figure out of the corner of my right eye. "What the..."

I spun towards it, shrieking a little as I saw a dirty looking figure with wild curly hair, grey from either dust or old age, which one I wasn't entirely certain.

Pippa stopped at the sound of my shriek, but it was too late. The old woman was already lunging towards her, rasping in a voice that sounded like it had been mixed with gravel. "What are you doing trespassing in my home?"

Pippa screamed as the body flung itself at her. I only saw the long yellowing fingernails clawing at her.

"Quick! Run!" I tried to call out. But running in that claustrophobic room was not easy and Pippa had stumbled awkwardly in the direction of the wall of newspaper.

Surprisingly agile, the woman jumped out of the way before the wall came down. It seemed like she was used to dodging this sort of thing, but Pippa was not so nimble and not so lucky.

At first, only the top few newspapers slipped off, but pretty soon it was an avalanche, and there was no stopping it. I lunged out of way myself, coughing violently as dirt and dust flung up into my nostrils.

My eyes were enveloped in dust, and I frantically tried to push it away, along with the stench that grew stronger with the figure's presence.

"Pippa!"

The dust settled and I raced over to her. The witch-like figure, a woman I could see now, had grey hair and wrinkled, leathery skin that she shielded from the light coming through from the front of the house.

I could only see her head staring out the top of the newspapers. "Please just answer me, say something, let me know that you are still alive."

"I'm alive," she muttered, "but I am going to kill you."

***

"Maureen, I think we ought to get you to a hospital."

She swatted at my hand and pulled her tattered

shawl tighter around her shoulders as she hobbled away. Her body was all pointy joints and angles, and I wondered how long it had been since she'd last eaten a proper meal.

"I think it's me that needs to get to a hospital," Pippa said, still brushing bits of dirt and debris off her body. "Or at least a hotel for a long hot bath." She shot me a pleading look.

"Are you talking to me then?" I asked her, hopeful at her not-entirely-homicidal tone.

"You mean after you almost got me crashed to death?"

But my attention was snatched away by Maureen who was sitting, shivering, on her own curb.

"Maureen," I said gently, sitting towards her. "We can get someone to help you, maybe some help cleaning your house out."

Pippa shot me a look and shook her head. "That's the worst thing you can say to a hoarder," she whispered to me. "You'll just make her panic."

"That's my collection," she finally said. Her proper speaking voice shocked me. I was expecting a raspy old drawl, but she had a prim and proper English accent with a clipped and pronounced delivery of every word. "And it is not to be touched."

I glanced at Pippa before turning my attention back to Maureen. "And was there something you were hoping to add to your collection, Maureen?"

She looked at me with sharp, bird-like features. I could see now that even though dirt covered her face, underneath it was a rather pretty face with well-defined, high cheekbones and piercing blue eyes. "To what precisely do you refer to?"

"A painting," I said softly, "of two young children. Twins, probably." I glanced up at Pippa and she seemed to understand precisely now why we were here. "Gus Sampson told me you were interested in buying it off him."

She cast me a long steely glare like I should already know the answer to the question, as though I was foolish for even asking.

"I did not want to buy that painting off him," she said in her short, clipped, posh tone that still didn't match her exterior. "That is my painting!"

"Your painting?" I whispered. "What do you mean, Maureen?"

"That is a painting of my two children," she whispered in a chilling tone. "The twins that I lost many years ago."

I sucked in a short gasp. "Maureen, I'm so sorry."

Pippa looked aghast. "So why won't Gus give it back to you then?" She glanced back over her shoulder at the house. Suddenly a lot of things about the place were starting to make sense.

"That old man refuses to part with it," Maureen whispered bitterly. "No matter what I try to do to get it back." She looked away, gazing off into the distance. In that moment, she was no longer sitting there with us, but was far away, lost in some deep, dark crevice of her past. "Why he won't part with it, I have no idea. That painting..." She stopped to close her eyes. "In all my years of collecting items, antiques, objects, storing everything I could get my hands on, that painting is the one thing I truly want, and the one thing I can't add to my collection."

I glanced up at Pippa. It seemed like Maureen had been collecting and hoarding everything she could find in some desperate attempt to replace what she had lost: her children.

"Maureen," Pippa said, joining us by the curb. "Do

you know why no one has ever purchased that painting before? There are rumors that it is haunted, and that anyone who buys it will be cursed."

Maureen opened her eyes and bit her lip. "That comes as no surprise to me. Rumors created by me in order to keep others away, and spread amongst others, no doubt. I had no idea that they would grow legs, but at least it means that I know where the painting is."

Pippa's face was a mixture of distress and disappointment. "I can't believe Gus would be so selfish as to keep the painting from you."

The faraway look returned to Maureen's eyes. "No matter what price I offer, he claims it is not enough. I have no idea why that man is so intent on keeping the one thing I have as a memory of my children." Her voice began to crack and Pippa reached her hand out to cover the old woman's.

"We'll get the painting back for you, I promise, Maureen," Pippa whispered.

But there was something I had to ask Maureen. "Why was Gus here, visiting you over the weekend?"

Maureen shook her head. "He was warning me to stay away from his shop," she whispered bitterly. "Had some crazy idea in his head that I had been snooping around, that I would try to break into the shop to take the painting away. That's why I was squirreled away today, hiding out the back. I was afraid he might return with more threats."

Again, there was something I had to ask. "And had you been, Maureen? Had you tried to break in, to find the painting?"

She shook her head. "I don't drive, dear, not with my eyesight. How could I get to Belldale on my own?" She turned and looked me straight in the eyes, then whispered, "But my great nephew lives there, and he has been trying to secure it for me. But with no luck."

Pippa and I were just staring at each other.

I knew we were both thinking the same thing, but it was Pippa who finally said it out loud. "Maureen, is your great nephew's name Romeo?"

Maureen frowned and shook her head. "No, dear. His name is George."

We both stared at each other, the disappointment between us palpable.

***

Pippa still desperately needed a bath and I needed a warm bed.

"So I guess that's how the whole curse rumor got started," Pippa murmured as we headed back towards the car. "I'm not sure whether the paranormal club is going to be exited to hear this news or disappointed by it."

"Disappointed that it wasn't a real curse?" I shrugged. "In a way, it was cursed. Just not caused by an evil spirit."

Pippa shivered and looked up at the dark clouds that were circling above. "Maureen's story doesn't explain everything, though. We still don't know who killed Jason or Bridget, or what the heck Gus was doing scaring us away that night. Or who Maureen's great nephew is."

I could feel a smile creeping its way to my lips. "Are you saying, Pippa, that you would *like* to know those things? Does this mean that you are back on the case?"

She let out a heavy sigh. "We always work better when we are together."

"In more ways than one."

I wrapped my arm around her neck and did a little hop and skip in mid-air. "I knew you would be interested when I finally got you out here. I'm sorry I tricked you, Pippa," I said as I stopped skipping. "Seriously. That was terrible of me. But come on, you have to admit it was more than worth it." I nodded towards the house. "If we hadn't come along then Maureen could have died in there."

Pippa looked back at the house and nodded. "She definitely could have been crushed to death. Like I almost was."

My mouth dropped open and I let out the loudest gasp I had ever heard.

All of a sudden, I knew.

I knew who had killed Jason and Bridget.

Chapter 11

Our weekend away turned into a single long day of driving. Pippa still hadn't gotten her bath.

"Do you think Maureen did it?" Pippa asked while she was huddled up beside me in the passenger seat. "Do you think she was trying to get her painting back? Or trying to teach Gus a lesson?"

The longer I drove, the less confident I was becoming in my theory. I closed my eyes for just a second (I was driving after all) and told myself that I needed to trust my instincts.

"No, I don't think Maureen did it," I said quietly. "I think she is just a heartbroken old lady, not a cold-blooded killer."

"Not a cold-blooded killer now, but she seems to hate Gus. What if she tried to break in to steal the painting, accidentally killed Jason and thought, well, if Gus gets blamed for it, that's just too bad?"

"And what about the second body? What about Bridget? Maureen was in her home in Pottsville when that happened."

"Oh." Pippa slunk back against her seat. "I forgot

about that." She was silent for a moment. "Then what are you thinking, Rachael?"

"I need to get inside Gus's shop again, while he isn't there, to see if I'm correct."

When Pippa didn't give me any sort of response, I glanced at her to get a good look at her face. She was staring out the window. "I don't think that's such a good idea."

"Oh, come on, Pippa. This isn't still about the curse, is it? We know how the rumor of the curse started now, and it was a very sad story indeed. You can't still believe that painting is haunted."

She had her face pressed so hard against the window that it was entirely smooshed. "Just because Maureen started the rumor," she murmured, "doesn't mean it's not true. In fact, having heard her story, it seems even more likely that the painting could be haunted." She looked down. "I didn't know that the twins in the painting were based on real people. Or that they had died a long time ago."

I opened my mouth to say something, but closed it again. With her head pressed up against the window like that, looking so forlorn, Pippa reminded me of a small child. I could tell that she was truly upset about

Maureen's revelation, so I spoke gently. "She's a grieving mother, Pippa. She hasn't cursed the painting."

Pippa finally lifted her head to stare at me. "What about all the weird things that have happened to you then, Rachael? Do you have an explanation for all of them?"

"Some of them, I do," I muttered. "And I'm sure there are perfectly logical explanations for the rest of them as well."

We drove the rest of the way in silence.

***

"Shoot, Gus is in the shop." I leaned forward for a second. It looked like he was finally making moves to clear his stuff out and the butterflies in my stomach began to do a dance. This could mean that the sale of the property might be back on the table. And I would have to make a very big decision.

I quickly turned my head away as I sat in my parked car, so that Gus wouldn't spot me staring straight at him.

"What do we do now?" I asked.

Pippa unclicked her seatbelt. "I'm still up for that bath."

"I know," I said, ignoring her. "We'll wait in the back, in secret, 'til he leaves, then break in just like we did the other day!"

Pippa was shaking her head vigorously. "No! No way! You can count me out."

I was shocked. "But, Pippa, I know what happened! Or at least I think I do!"

"I don't care, Rachael! I may be back on the case, but I can't pick another lock! I am trying to stay out of trouble from now on. I don't need an arrest on my record. Another one, I mean."

I wondered if 'stay out of trouble' also meant staying away from the paranormal society. I had noticed a distinct change in her demeanor since our visit to Maureen's. Even though she was still talking about the curse, I could sense that she was ready to give up the ghost, so to speak. And I couldn't wait for her to come back down to earth.

But I desperately needed her lock-picking skills. Just one last time.

"Let's at least go into the bakery instead of just

sitting here," Pippa said. "We should at least check that Bronson is doing okay."

We each spilled through the doors and I thought Bronson looked slightly disappointed to see us. He was probably looking forward to an entire weekend in charge with the bosses away. "Ignore us," I said quickly as Pippa and I hurried into the kitchen. "Trip got cut short...long story." I glanced at the clock: 3:30. This day felt like the longest day of my life.

Bronson surprised me by following us into the kitchen. "Actually, I'm kinda glad you guys are back. We got a huge booking for this afternoon, short notice, and I'm not sure I can handle it all on my own. It's a birthday party. Apparently, the restaurant they were supposed to have it at flooded. I didn't want to have to tell them no." He glanced at the two of us, waiting for direction.

Pippa looked at me. "Can you put this mystery on ice for the afternoon? We need the cash, considering how quiet it's been recently."

Which one of us was the boss again? The lines had definitely become muddied. "Yes, Bronson," I said. "We can help out a bit." I caught the look on Pippa's face. "But please tend to the front counter while the two of us are out here. Thank you."

"Come on, Pips, you're the only person I know with nimble enough fingers to be able to pick a lock quickly." I shut the kitchen door so that Bronson couldn't overhear us.

"Don't try to butter me up." She nodded towards a tray of cookies. "Speaking of which, these probably need to go out on display. And, if you're done playing detective for the day, you could actually help me out with this party we're now supposed to be catering. I would really appreciate the help. Can't you just forget about this whole thing for one day?"

I picked up the tray and swallowed. I glanced over my shoulder in the direction of Gus's store. All I wanted to do was go over there and prove my theory correct. I knew Pippa and Bronson would be able to handle the function without me.

"Rach?"

Suddenly, there was the sound of a heavy thud and the front doors were pushed open as party guest began to spill in. I grabbed a donut and scarfed it down for a bit of energy.

I nodded. "I will stay and help, Pippa. Of course I will."

But half an hour into the function, my stomach seemed to have other plans. There was a smashing sound as I dropped the tray I was carrying and keeled over in pain. Clutching my stomach, I whispered for Pippa, who came running over to me. "Oh no. All my brownies, ruined on the floor!" I cried out.

"Don't worry about that, you knucklehead! Bronson, take over while I drive Rachael to the hospital! We'll be back before the end of the function. I hope!"

He nodded and threw down the cloth he'd been drying his hands with. "Can do, miss! You'd better go quick. She looks terrible."

"Thanks," I croaked. "Don't go asking me for a raise any time soon."

***

"How long do blood test results take?" I groaned, shielding my eyes from the glare of the fluorescent lights. My stomachache had subsided a little, like it always seemed to after an hour or so, but my entire body was aching. I began to imagine the absolute worst-case scenario. I'd had these aches and pains for weeks—or was it months—and that couldn't have been good.

The doctor was a chipper young woman named Doctor Shu Ng, who I quite liked, even though she was probably about to tell me I was dying.

"Well, Miss Robinson, you're not going to like the results much, I don't think, considering your line of work."

I could feel my eyes growing wide. "Oh no, what is it? Am I going to become paralyzed? Lose the use of my arms?" I leaned forward. "Be straight with me, doc, will I ever bake again?"

She allowed a smile of amusement to cross her face. "It's not as severe as all that. Yes, you'll be able to bake again. But as for how many of the items you'll be able to eat, that's another story."

I frowned and tilted my head. "You're going to have to be less cryptic, doc."

"You've got a gluten allergy. Quite a bad one, I'm afraid." She raised an eyebrow at me. "Are your symptoms worse after you eat one of your cakes, for instance?"

I thought back over my symptoms over the past few weeks. "Yes," I gasped. "It seems worst after I've eaten a piece of cake or a brownie." I threw my head back. "Oh, why did this have to happen to me!" I was half-joking, being melodramatic for the sake of it, but there was an element of truth to my dismay.

Pippa looked at me in horror. "Oh my goodness, Rachael, what are you going to do?"

I thought about all those gluten-free items I had bought the other day when I'd been fibbing to Pippa about what I was up to. I gulped. Maybe the only thing I was cursed with was bad karma...or irony.

"We might have to add a few new items to the menu, Pips." I sighed. "Or else, I'm going to have to leave the majority of the taste-testing to you."

She was trying not to smile. "I think I can handle that."

Doctor Ng gave me some tips and some brochures, and told me to see my personal physician for more blood tests and advice if my symptoms got any worse. "Feel better soon, Rachael."

"I hate to ask you this, Rach, but do you think you

could come back and help out at the function?" Pippa cringed apologetically as she waited for my answer.

I was weary and ragged, but I managed a smile. "Just try to keep me away."

***

"Shoot, sorry, Bronson. That took way longer than we thought," I said, rushing into the bakery. My stomach was rumbling again already and I instinctively reached for a brownie before Pippa smacked it out of my hand.

"Oh, right."

The man who was apparently in charge of organizing the birthday party, a 40-something year old man with an expensive suit and a matching attitude, marched over and asked who was in charge.

"That would be me, I guess."

He hesitated before he handed the check over. "We were expecting a far bigger venue than this. Something twice the size, in fact."

When I'd updated the website to include our new function facility, I'd assumed I'd have Gus's shop to expand into by now. I really needed to log in and fix that up.

Pippa and I exchanged glances. "We may be small in size, but that just adds to the cozy atmosphere! I'm sure your guests have all been able to get nice and close to each other. It would have made for some great socializing!"

Bronson nodded. "And everyone looks more than happy, sir."

The man looked a little skeptical, but he nodded and handed over the check. "I suppose that's true," he said. "Thanks, girls."

I heaved a heavy sigh of relief. I needed that check. Mostly so I could pay Pippa a big fat bonus at the end of the month.

We high-fived. "Thank God today is all over with. Hey, Rach, promise me one thing?"

"Anything."

"No more high-maintenance clients."

Now that was a promise I could keep. "Deal."

We both stared at the rows of leftovers. Pippa picked up a brownie and began to hand it to me before she realized what she was doing. Looked like we both needed to get used to my new dietary restrictions. "Oh. Shoot, Rach, I'm sorry. What are you going to do?"

I laughed. "You mean what am I going to eat from now on? I know it does sound crazy, but I have heard of people that eat foods besides cakes and cookies and donuts."

Pippa's eyes were wide. "That's no way to live. We are going to have to start stocking a very wide range of gluten-free products. Otherwise, you're going to starve to death."

I chuckled. I could deal with my gluten allergy later. Right then, I was just grateful that Pippa and I were back to being best friends again.

I took a deep breath. "Now, Pippa, if I could just ask you one big favor..."

***

"Okay, but I swear this is the last time I'm doing this." Pippa's tone was teasing as she reached for the pin in her hair.

"Maybe it's the last time I'm going to need you to do this. After all this, I'm thinking about giving up the detective work for good."

Pippa's hands worked expertly and soon the lock clicked open. The sun had set and the shop was empty.

I took a deep breath. There was only one thing left to do.

Chapter 12

"Why does he still keep this here?" Pippa whispered. It was the first time she had really come face to face with the painting, the first time she had not been completely afraid to.

"Even after he started clearing the other stuff out of here," I said quietly. "And why won't he give the painting back to Maureen?"

I knelt down. "Come have a look at this, Pippa."

She squatted down besides me. "Those are definitely wires." I ran the thin metal wire through my hands, letting them snake through my fingers.

I stood up again. "In the dark we wouldn't have seen them, of course. That night when Gus was trying to scare us away."

"What was he trying to scare us away from, though?" Pippa asked.

"From this." I pushed the painting aside.

"Holy crud!" Pippa exclaimed. What are those?"

The sound of the back door opening made both of us jump and I quickly put the painting back in position.

I grabbed Pippa and pulled her so that we were huddled behind an old statue that wouldn't stop wobbling. "Keep still or it is going to topple over," I whispered to her.

A large white figure that looked like it was floating came towards us and Pippa's knees only started jittering more and more.

"I can't...I can't stop shaking, Rach. I knew...I knew this place was haunted...and now the ghost has come looking for us!"

She made a move to run, but I pulled her back and reached for the flashlight she had dropped on the floor last time, which was still lying there, out of place amongst the expensive old relics.

Pippa was going to give away our position anyway.

I flicked the light on and shone it on the hazy white figure lunging towards us. "There's your ghost," I said.

"Romeo?" Pippa's breathing was short and ragged. "What are you doing? Did you break in here?"

"No," I said firmly. "Because he has a key."

"What?" Pippa whispered. "Romeo, what's going on?"

He gulped and glanced towards the painting. And

what was behind it.

He kicked the painting so hard that the frame split and cracked, causing both Pippa and I to gasp. While we both lunged towards it to check it was still intact, the statue smashed down around us and Romeo fled out the back door, kicking and knocking items over as he went, creating a gauntlet for Pippa and I to get through if we were ever going to catch him.

"Stop him!" I yelled.

Pippa tripped over the statue and cried out in pain, clutching her ankle. "Pippa!?" I knelt down beside her while she groaned for me to go after Romeo. "That is his stuff hidden behind the painting, isn't it?"

I nodded at her. "Did you ever ask who Romeo was when you first met him? Pippa, he wasn't just a customer here that day you two met. He *worked* here."

Pippa groaned in pain again. "You have to go after him. He's going to get away. He's going to get away with killing Jason and Bridget."

"But, Pippa..."

"I'm fine," she insisted. "You can come back for me later. Hurry, go!"

I took off after Romeo. Outside, it was already dark

and I immediately wished I'd thought to bring the flashlight. I turned back so that I could run and get it, but a hand reached out and grabbed me. I kicked at him. "Let me go!"

"Not if you're going to go back in there and reveal my secret." He placed his hands over my mouth. "Not if you're going to go back in there and tell Pippa."

I stopped struggling for a second. "What?"

I heard him gulp. "I don't want Pippa to know what I did."

"It's too late for that now, Romeo. She already knows. She already saw the stolen antique swords you are hiding in there." I swallowed. "I know that Gus would never put his business in jeopardy that way." I pulled hard and finally freed myself, but he grabbed me again by the wrist.

"Pippa is lying in there hurt, Romeo. If you care about her at all, you will let me go in and see her. What if one of your swords falls on her and hurts her, or worse, kills her the way they killed Jason and Bridget."

Romeo brought his hands to his face and stumbled forward as a sob escaped from his lungs. "I never meant for any of this to happen."

I yanked my wrist free. "You could have stopped it, Romeo. You could have stopped it after the first time. What the heck are you doing, keeping those things stored there?"

I heard him sniffling. Not so tough once he'd been caught. "There's a black market for them," he whispered. "When I moved back to town a month or two ago, I got into contact with some people who were interested in buying them."

"So what happened?" I asked. "How was Jason killed?"

Romeo hesitated at first, but then came clean. "It was a deal gone bad. The sword he wanted had been stolen from some history museum. I didn't steal it. I was just the middleman. When he came in to buy it from me, he got aggressive and I was afraid he was going to walk out with the sword without paying. I tried to get it back from him, but..." He stared off into the distance and I could tell he was picturing it all in his mind. "The sword was heavy," he said, shaking his head. "I couldn't control it. The next thing I knew, he was on the floor. It all happened so fast."

"What about Bridget?" I asked, not picturing her as the type who would be interested in black market swords.

Romeo sighed. "I hid the swords in my apartment until after the cops searched the antique store. When I thought it was safe, I brought them back to the shop to hide them. I knew that if I hid them behind that bloody painting that everyone is so afraid of, no one would ever see them there. No one would dare to move the painting. Not even my old man."

I narrowed my eyes. "But someone did move the painting, didn't they?"

Romeo nodded. "That lady, Bridget, she moved it and..." He couldn't finish his sentence.

"One of the swords fell on her," I said quietly.

Romeo nodded.

"What the heck are you two doing out here?" I jumped at the sound of Gus's voice.

I spun to face him. "Gus, I'm just..." I turned back to Romeo. "How could you do this to your dad?"

"I did this FOR my dad," Romeo cried. "The business was failing. This was my way of bringing in extra money for him. I was protecting him by not telling him about it...not telling him where the swords were stored."

I could see Gus's face growing heavy. "You did know,

didn't you?" I whispered.

He was still staring at the ground. "Of course I did. After that young man was killed, I found the swords and told Romeo to get out of my house and my business. He already had that new job next door with you anyway. Which he managed to mess up after a week! Like he always manages to do!"

Romeo took an angry step towards his father. "I was just trying to help you! You could at least show a little gratitude!"

"Help me? By completely destroying the business that I worked all my life to build? By killing a person in my store? Why should I be grateful for that! You should be grateful I tried to protect you instead of turning you in to the cops! But then you had to go and put the swords back there while I was out of town for the weekend! Which I had to rush back to remedy! Just like I've always had to clean up all your messes!"

Romeo raised his fist and took a step towards his dad, ready and aimed. I sucked in a sharp breath, shielding my face as Romeo prepared to strike.

Just then sirens sounded and Pippa came hobbling out of the back of the shop. "You may as well keep your hands up, Romeo! Because you're about to be arrested!

Not only are you the worst boyfriend and employee I've ever seen, you're the worst criminal as well."

***

Detective Crawford shoved Romeo into the back of the van while Jackson kept the engine running.

After a moment of hesitation, Detective Crawford strode over to me. "I've only got a moment. I just wanted to tell you that we found that missing video footage from your store. A young man confessed to breaking in and stealing it. Name of George Tatler. He said he was trying to catch an art thief or something. Thought something strange was going on at Gus's place. A very convoluted story about an old painting. I dunno, just between you and I, he was a little eccentric. Some stuff about a curse." She gave me an 'I don't know what to tell you' face.

"Another amateur detective, I guess."

Detective Crawford nodded at me and turned to leave. "Hey," she said. "Thanks for your help solving this case, Rachael." I nodded and caught Jackson's eye briefly as she jumped back into the car.

We exchanged nothing but a brief smile as they drove away.

Once again, I was left on the curbside with Gus Sampson as my only companion. Pippa had had the longest day of her life and she'd passed out with exhaustion in the back seat of my car.

"Gus, why did you do all this? Why did you cover for Romeo?" I stared out into the black night. "Why did you let everyone believe all the stupid superstitious stuff?"

"Because I was so desperate to save my shop, I would rather the police look for a killer on the loose, or the community blame a ghost, than blame my son and put us all out of business." Gus picked up a stick and dug it into the concrete.

"That night when Pippa and I..." I paused. "Broke in. That was you, wasn't it, trying to scare us away?"

Gus nodded reluctantly. "I used the curse to try and scare you away, get you off Romeo's trail. I already knew a little bit about the curse, of course, but Romeo told me all this extra stuff that little blue-haired friend of yours knew about it. All these details I never heard before. All came from some paranormal society or something."

I sighed and shook my head. "It all became a bit of a

self-fulfilling prophecy, I think."

I turned to face Gus. "So why wouldn't you give the painting back to Maureen?" I lowered my voice and spoke softly. "You know what that painting means to her, right? What the painting depicts?"

Gus dropped his head and nodded. "Yeah, I know. But if I gave the painting back, then I wouldn't have anything to attract customers, would I? I know the police would never take the curse theory seriously, but if enough regular people could be fooled... Well, people are interested in that sort of stuff.

"But you wouldn't stop snooping," he huffed.

I stood up. "Well, Gus, you can't put everything right. But there is one thing you can do."

He nodded. "I know," he whispered.

***

Pippa collapsed into my bed. I was going to take the sofa that night. "I can't believe all this time, there really was no curse. I guess you probably think I really am stupid and easily taken in now."

I sat down besides her and gave her a tiny wink. "At least, no curse that we know of for certain."

She gave me an amused, slacked jawed look and sat up. "You gotta be kidding me, Rachael. Our roles really have reversed now!"

I sat and thought for a moment. "There really is a lot we don't know about. I keep thinking of all those stories your friends told that night at the meeting. There really are a lot of unsolved mysteries in Belldale."

Pippa laid her head back against the pillow. "Does this mean that you will come to another meeting?"

I thought about it for a moment. "I think I might have to. After all, I'm going to need another mystery to solve now, aren't I?"

Epilogue

Two months later.

I tapped my champagne flute with my spoon. "Now," I said as the chatter died down. "I've already had one grand opening three years ago, but this feels like another big moment. A second grand opening." I nodded at Pippa, who ran to pull down the curtain.

"Ta da!"

"Ladies and gentlemen, can I present to you: Rachael's Boutique Bakery, part two!"

The crowd clapped and Jackson, stranded amongst them, caught my eye and winked at me. "Congrats," he mouthed, before he turned his attention back to Detective Crawford.

Gus slowly walked up to me and extended his hand. "Congratulations, Rachael. I mean it."

I grinned at him. "I'm just glad that the sewing shop on the other side decided to sell up! So it was great timing for both of us. How is your store going, anyway?"

Gus nodded. "It's still a little slow, as you can

understand. But since I've started to move into restoration, things have picked up a little." He suddenly grew very serious. "Rachael, if you have a moment in the midst of all your celebrations, can I borrow you for a minute?"

I nodded and asked Pippa to supervise as I followed him into his store. No longer dark and drab, it was bright and airy, with fresh coats of white and yellow paint that made the whole place look light and inviting. "You can see all the artwork I'm restoring now."

I nodded, slowly walking along the rows of paintings. "I'm a little surprised, after all…"

"Miss Robinson?" a posh English voice interrupted.

I spun around to see Maureen Tatler standing there.

"This is why I invited you over, Rachael. I think you ought to be here when I present this."

Gus reached behind his counter and pulled out the painting of the twins. The broken frame was now replaced with fine silver, the ripped canvas painstakingly put back together, and the ruined paint restored back to its original quality.

Maureen's eyes filled with tears as she took the painting from him with shaking hands.

"My collection is finally complete after all these years," she whispered, running her withered hand over the painting, gently caressing the faces of the twins, lost in a cloud of memories.

Back at the bakery, I closed the door quietly behind me.

"Pippa," I called out quietly with a small grin. "Come here. I want to ask you something."

"What is it, Rach?"

"Since we are expanding, I want to give you a promotion: to head manager, equal with me."

She reached over and squeezed my arm. "Nah," Pippa said. "I appreciate the offer so much, Rach, you know that, but you know it's not like me to stick around in one job for too long. Sorry to say this, Rach, but I just booked a ticket for a paranormal mystery tour of the midwest with the paranormal society, so I'm not gonna be around for a while!"

My face fell a little. "But when will you be back?"

"In a few months! Don't worry, though, I'll be back before you know it. But I'll probably look for a new job when I get back. Change is good for the soul."

I nodded. "Well, good luck, Pips. I'm going to miss

you. But I understand."

As the party continued, and guests ate and socialized, I moved towards the window. Maureen Tatler was hobbling to her car with the painting under her arm.

"Here, let me help you," I said, slightly out of breath from running to catch up with her.

"Thank you, deary," she said, climbing in to the passenger side. I nodded to the driver, her great nephew George.

Maureen grabbed my arm with her bony fingers just as I was turning to walk away.

"The curse is lifted now, Rachael."

Thank You!

Thanks for reading *Donuts, Antiques and Murder*. I hope you enjoyed reading the story as much as I enjoyed writing it. If you did, it would be awesome if you left a review for me on Amazon and/or Goodreads.

If you would like to know about all my new releases and have the opportunity to get free books, make sure you sign up for our Cozy Mystery Newsletter.

FairfieldPublishing.com/cozy-newsletter

On the next page, I have included a preview of my next book, *Death by Chocolate Cake*. It will be available on Amazon in May 2016.

I am also including a preview of the first cozy mystery from my friend Miles Lancaster. I really hope you like it!

Stacey Alabaster

Preview: Death by Chocolate Cake

Summertime had taken all of Belldale into its warm embrace. People were, in general, jollier at this time of year, the sun and heat making them lazier and less likely to stress out.

And less likely to commit murder. Belldale had been at peace for almost six months. No strange activity, no paranormal sightings, and no unexplained deaths.

It would almost have been boring if we weren't all in such cheerful moods. Summer was a good time of year for the hospitality business and everyone on our little food strip was doing a banging trade, especially my shop, "Rachael's Boutique Bakery."

Which was why I was hesitant to leave it behind to go shoot a TV program for three months.

"I'll be fine! Of course you can leave me in charge!" Pippa squealed after I told her the news back in my apartment. "Rachael, there's no way you are missing this opportunity." She squealed again and clapped her hands.

"Okay, okay..." I said, giggling a little. "Calm down though, I haven't made it through the final judges' audition yet."

"Oh, you will though!" Pippa grabbed my hands and started jumping up and down. She was clearly still on a post-nuptial high. And I had to admit her newly rejuvenated enthusiasm for life was rubbing off on me, even though I was still skeptical about the stranger who was waiting in the next room.

"Where is he going to...fit?" I whispered, peering out the door. All I could see was the back of Marcello's head, all dark curls.

Pippa shrugged. "He's just going to have to snuggle up on the sofa with me!"

"...right."

It wasn't the right time to have a talk about her maybe finding her own place and moving out, though I knew that moment would have to come.

I heard something breaking in the kitchen. "Oh," Pippa said, making a face. "Sorry about that. He's a little clumsy. But that's all part of his charm." She patted me on the arm. "You'll get used to it. After all, we're going to get very cozy, the three of us living here in this one apartment!"

169

I took a deep breath and smiled at her. "Yes, we are."

There was another crashing sound, followed by a loud, "Sorry about that!"

I wondered how much sleep I was actually going to get.

***

"Honey. You look terrible. Straight into makeup. That should take care of most of it." Justin shoved me towards a makeshift tent that was brimming with men and women in black shirts holding panels of powders and bronzers and looking even less awake then I was.

"Remember, we want her looking twenty-two!"

It was a long morning. And I mean LONG. When it was finally time for me to scurry my way past the line of hopefuls that thought they actually had a chance of making it onto the show, I felt like I was going to keel over. Two hours was the amount of sleep I'd gotten the night before. And right then I was running on caffeine and Justin's barking orders.

"Now," he said, brushing my hair off my shoulder and examining my face in his hands. "Do you remember what you have to tell the judges?"

I nodded groggily. "I'm twenty...two..."

Justin nodded. "What else."

"I own my own bakery. Baking has been my passion since I was a little girl. I baked my first cake when I was only three..."

Justin let out a long sigh.

"What?" I asked, a little offended.

"It's just not...very exciting, is it?" He waved his hand in the direction of the crowd that lay outside the studio. "I mean, that might pass for excitement in this place, but it just doesn't make for very compelling TV, does it, darling?" Another sigh. "Are you sure there's nothing else interesting about you, honey?" He looked upwards and clucked his tongue. "Maybe we can make something up. Did you parents die when you were very young?"

"No!" I said. "And I'm not going to pretend they did. It's gotta be bad karma or something."

"Well, we have to think of something quick." He dared a look inside the judge's room. "Something that's going to impress them."

"What about my baking?" I asked, as though that should be the obvious answer. "I thought I was supposed to impress them with my super skills in the kitchen. Isn't that kind of the point of the show?"

Justin laid a hand on my shoulder and shook his head slowly. "Oh, sweetie, you really have no idea how this TV thing works, do you?" He consulted a list on his tablet. "Maybe you're a lost cause. One of these other guys might have an interesting back story...maybe something tragic in their past that we can get them to open up about."

"Wait!" I placed a hand on top of his tablet. "I do have an interesting sort of hobby," I said reluctantly.

There was a slight glimmer of interest in Justin's eyes. "Go on."

I took a deep breath and quickly told him everything that had happened in Belldale over the past year: the three deaths, the paranormal mysteries, and my part in solving the cases.

Justin's jaw was wide open by the time I'd finished. "Now, why didn't you lead with that?" He placed a gentle hand on my shoulder and guided me to the judging room before lowering his voice. "I had no idea this town was so interesting. Huh. I've only been here a couple of days and I almost died of boredom."

"Yeah, well, it's definitely not boring all the time."

He raised an eyebrow. "I guess I just came at the wrong time of year then."

I shifted uncomfortably. "Things have been peaceful here recently. I don't want to jinx it. Besides..." I trailed off, a little reluctant to continue.

"Besides what?"

I shrugged. "All the deaths and stuff kind of gave the town a bad rap. I don't think certain members of the police force would like me bringing all that stuff up on national TV."

I could see the glimmer in Justin's eyes growing stronger. "Oh, honey," he said. "What 'certain members'? A man, I take it." He shot me a knowing look. "One that you like."

"No," I said quickly, wrapping my arms across my chest. "I just want to respect their wishes."

Justin nodded. "Don't worry, honey, I understand. We won't sensationalize anything." Then, into his walkie-talkie, he announced my audition number and name to the judges. "Up next we've got, Rachael. Belldale's very own number one Murder Expert!"

"Justin!"

There were three of them.

I tried to focus on the "nice" judge, a blonde lady named Dawn who was nearing the end of middle age. She was known for giving the contestants constructive, rather than downright vicious, critiques. And I tried to ignore the glares of Pierre, the judge who was known for giving no holds barred criticism and occasionally reducing contestants to tears with his caustic barbs. Not that it dulled his popularity. Of the three judges, he was by far the most famous and the most beloved on social media.

Then there was Wendy. Nobody really paid much attention to her.

"Go on, dear, tell us a little about yourself," Dawn encouraged. "What is all this stuff about murders we've been hearing so much about?"

"I, erm..." I caught Justin's glare out of the corner of my eye. "Don't stammer," he had told me.

"Why don't you try one of my cakes?"

I turned around to fetch the cakes I'd prepared the day before but which the producers made to look like I'd baked that day. I knew the judges had already tasted them the day before and made up their minds, but we had to go through the motions.

"Delicious," Wendy said, pushing her long dark hair out of her face. "Wouldn't change a thing, darling!"

A nice, but fairly hollow--and, let's face it, useless-- comment.

I focused on Pierre, who screwed his face up as he slowly chewed the cream cake I had presented him with. I wondered why he had to make such a show of it when he already knew what it tasted like and already knew what he was going to say.

He finally placed his napkin down and swallowed. Then he stared straight at me for a good ten seconds before he finally delivered his verdict.

"That was...fine," he said. Non-plussed. No expression on his face except a dead stare. "Tell me, Rachael, why you deserve to be on Baking Warriors over the thousands of auditonees outside?"

The nine other audtionees, I thought. But with his stare on me, I was in no state to be smart with him. Or even to defend myself.

"I...I...um, I've been baking since I was three years old," I said rather meekly. "It's...it is my passion...."

Pierre leaned back and shook his head. I saw his gesture for a producer, then heard him whisper, "Can we use any of the murder stuff?"

Justin shrugged. "If she gets through." He shot me a look over his shoulder then returned to Pierre. "Though I really don't think she will. Shall I bring in the next contestant?"

Pierre nodded. "I've had enough of this one."

"Thank you for you time," I said softly before Justin led me swiftly out of the room and told me to return to the green room. I didn't even get to hear Dawn's verdict.

I was red-faced and annoyed by the time Justin finally joined me for a debrief. He just shrugged. "It's dog eat dog, honey. You should have led with the murder stuff."

I sat down on a soggy sofa. "I'd rather not get through than use any of that stuff." I was aware that I was acting sulky but it had been a long day and I just wanted to go home. "I don't know why I'm still here. I obviously didn't get in."

Justin sighed and looked down on me in pity. "Look," he said. "Just between you and me, you're still in with a shot. A good shot. Look, I do NOT say this to everyone..." He lowered his voice. "But you are going through to the next round. Just sit tight and relax. You look good on camera and the judges really liked your cakes. That's all there is to it."

I looked up at him in shock. "But Pierre didn't seem impressed at all!"

Justin waved his hand dismissively. "Oh, that's all just for TV, honey. Pierre's the executive producer. If he likes you, you'll go through. Just relax. Have something to drink." He fetched some wine out of a cooler.

"No, thanks. I'm afraid if I drink I'll fall asleep."

"Come on, just a little sip! Honey, you'll have to start drinking if you get into TV."

I reluctantly accepted half a glass.

Just as Justin was plugging the cork back into the bottle a high-pitched squeal sounded from the direction of the judging room.

Justin let out a loud, exaggerated sigh that said, "I don't get paid enough for this." He threw the wine bottle back in the cooler. "Probably a rejected contestant. Or a judge who hasn't got their lunch on time. Wait here while I deal with it. I won't be a minute."

But Justin was way longer than a minute. After ten minutes had passed and Justin hadn't returned, I started to get worried.

Then I saw the ambulance.

"Are you okay?" I said, running towards a stricken-looking Justin with his headpiece in his hands. "What on earth has happened?"

Justin, white as a sheet, slowly looked over his shoulder and, with a trembling voice, simply said, "Pierre's dead, Rachael. Somebody killed him."

Thanks for reading a sample of *Death by Chocolate Cake*. I really hope you liked it. It will be available on Amazon in May, 2016.

Stacey Alabaster

Preview: Murder in the Mountains

Screams were not a normal part of the workday at Aspen Breeze. When Jennifer heard the anguished cry of the maid, she ran around the desk and sprinted out the door. Clint, not through with his breakfast, followed at her heels. The door to the room had been left open. The maid stood on the thick burgundy carpet in front of the unmade bed and pointed at the hot tub.

Water remained in the tub, but it wasn't swirling. The occupant, a red-haired, slightly chubby man whose name Jennifer had forgotten, was face down. His blue running shorts had changed to a darker blue due to dampness. Reddish colorations marred his throat. Another dark spot of blood mixed with hair around his right temple. Pale red splotches marred the water.

For a moment, she felt like the ground had opened and she had fallen into blackness. Legs weakened. Knees buckled. She shook her head and a few incoherent syllables came from her mouth. Clint's arm grasped her around her waist.

"Step back. It's okay," he said.

It was a silly thing to say, he later thought. Clearly, it was not okay, but in times of stress people will often say and do stupid things.

He eased her backward, and then sat her down on the edge of the bed. He walked back and took a second look at the hot tub. He had seen dead bodies when he covered the police beat. It wasn't a routine occurrence, but he had stood in the rain twice and on an asphalt pavement once as EMTs covered a dead man and lifted him into an ambulance.

By the time he turned around, Jennifer was back on her feet and the color had returned to her cheeks.

She patted her maid on the shoulder. "Okay, it's all right. We have to call the police. You can go, Maria. Go to the office and lay down."

"Yes, ma'am."

She glanced at Clint and saw he had his cell phone out.

"...at the Aspen Breeze Lodge," he was saying. "There's a dead body in Unit Nine. It doesn't look like it was a natural death." He nodded then slipped the cell phone in his pocket. "They said the chief was out on a call but should be here within fifteen minutes."

"Good." Jennifer put her hands on her hips. Her gaze stared toward the hot tub. A firm, determined tone came back in her voice.

"Clint, those marks on his throat. The red on his forehead. This wasn't an accident, was it?"

"We can't really say for sure. He might have tripped and hit...." The words withered in the face of her laser stare. "I doubt it. I...I really can't say for sure but...I doubt it."

They looked at one another for a few seconds. Light yellow flames rose up from the artificial fireplace and the crackling of wood sounded from the flames. Jennifer sighed. She realized there was nothing to do except wait for the police.

The silence was interrupted by a tall, thin man, unshaven as yet, who rushed in.

"Bill, what are you doing with the door open? It's still cold...." He stopped as if hit by a stun gun. Eyes widened. He stumbled but caught himself before he fell to the carpeted floor. "Oh, no! What happened?"

Jennifer shifted into her professional tone as manager. "We don't know yet, sir. I assume you knew this man."

He nodded weakly. "Yeah, Bill's been a friend of mine for years."

"I remember you from when you checked in yesterday, but I'm sorry I can't remember your name."

"Dale Ramsey."

Ramsey had a thin, pale face that flashed even paler. There was a chair close to him and he collapsed in it. He had an aquiline nose and chin but curly brown hair. His hand went to his heart.

"Sorry you had to learn about your friend's death this way, Mr. Ramsey," Jennifer said. "I regret to say I've forgotten his name too."

"Bill Hamilton."

Jennifer turned back to Clint. "Do you think we should move the body? Put it on the rug and cover it with a blanket?"

Clint shook his head. "I think the police would prefer it stay right where it is, at least for now."

Jennifer nodded. A steel gaze came in her eyes. She looked at Ramsey, who almost flinched. Then he shook slightly as if dealing with the aftermath of a panic attack.

"Mr. Ramsey, I am the owner of this Lodge and obviously I am very upset someone used it as a place for murder. So I trust you won't mind if I ask you a few questions - just to aid the police, of course."

Ramsey swallowed, or tried to. It looked like a rock had lodged in his throat. "Of course not. I...I do will anything I can to help," he said.

"Six single individuals checked into my lodge last night. That's a little unusual. I was commenting on that to Clint just last night. Now it turns out that you knew the deceased. Do you know the other four people who checked in?"

"Yes...I...yes."

There was a pause and Jennifer noted the look of sadness in his eyes.

"I realize you are upset, Mr. Ramsey, so just relax and take your time."

"We are all members of the Centennial Historical Society. All of us are history buffs," he finally answered.

"Why did you all check in here?"

Ramsey shifted in his chair. "This may sound unbelievable."

"Let's try it and see," Jennifer said.

"About a hundred and twenty-five years ago there was a Wells Fargo gold shipment in these parts. An outlaw gang headed by a man nicknamed The Falcon stole it. He got the name because he liked heights and the Rocky Mountains and had actually trained a falcon at one time. Rumor is, the gang got about a hundred thousand worth in gold, coins and bars. What's known is the gang drifted apart and a few members got shot, but the gold was never found. We believe it's buried very close by, up in the Rocky Mountain National Forest."

Jennifer nodded. The entrance to the forest was less than five miles from Aspen Breeze. All drivers had to do was turn left when they left the lodge and they would hit the entrance in about ten minutes.

"The Rocky Mountain National Forest is a huge area, thousands of miles there of virtually unexplored wilderness. You better have a specific location or you'll spend your lifetime looking and never find anything," she said.

'We have researched this gang for years. We think we know approximately where the gold was buried. It's more than just recovering the gold. This would be a historical find of enormous significance. We were going up there today to try to find the site."

"Maybe someone didn't want to share," Clint said.

Ramsey shook his head. "I doubt it. I've known these people for years. I don't think anyone would kill Bill. Besides, whoever it was would have to kill all of us too if he wanted to keep the gold to himself. Bill was in the high tech field, lower management, but he also liked the wilderness. He knew this forest better than any of us. We were counting on him to help find the site of the gold. He had searched the forest a number of times during the past five years.

I came out with him a few times. He thought he knew where the outlaws had hid their stash. He shared his opinions with us, but he was the one with the most expertise. Eddie, Eddie Tercelli, one of our group, is the second most knowledgeable about the location. He was out a few times too with Bill searching. But it would be tough for him to find the place on his own."

A blue light waved and flickered in the room. They heard a car door open and then slam shut. They looked up as the officer walked in. He wore a fine, crisp blue uniform with a bright silver badge. He had a slight paunch over his belt, but it didn't make him look old or slow. The intense gray eyes under the rim of the black police cap took in everything. His revolver was clearly visible on his right hip.

"Chief Sandish," Clint said, nodding.

Thanks for reading a sample of my first book, *Murder in the Mountains*. I really hope you liked it.

It will be available on Amazon in April, 2016.

Miles Lancaster

CPSIA information can be obtained at www.ICGtesting.com
Printed in the USA
LVOW07s2332140916

504664LV00001B/13/P

9 781533 315168